# WIDOWS' PLIGHT

One would think that two elderly ladies, reluctant pensioners on a younger generation, would be defenseless. But Kate Barsony and Addie Prentice had resources of courage and determination that were to surprise assorted tough characters.

It all began when Kate's handsome son-in-law was murdered. Although Jancsi, her lovely daughter, knew more about it than she would tell, it soon became evident that Jancsi and Addie's son, Lindsey, were mixed up in a vicious blackmail scheme that threatened all of them.

It was hard for Addie to picture Lindsey, a conscientious high school teacher, as part of blackmail. But she began to suspect that "Fix," the disbarred lawyer who had once come to see him, had something to do with it. As she ferreted out more of the sordid story, she began getting too close to the truth to suit certain underworld characters. And for the first time in her life Addie found that the world wasn't nearly so safe a place as she had imagined. . . .

*Scene: New York City*

*This novel has not appeared in any form prior to book publication.*

# RUTH FENISONG

# WIDOWS'

# PLIGHT

*Doubleday & Company, Inc., Garden City, New York*

BY RUTH FENISONG

*All of the characters in this book are fictitious, and any resemblance to actual persons, living or dead, is purely coincidental.*


*Printed in the United States of America*

# WIDOWS' PLIGHT

# 1

Every afternoon, short of snow or rain, Mrs. Addie Prentice escaped to Central Park. The strangers she met in the park were the only people within her sphere who seemed to welcome or even tolerate the sound of her voice. But on this March day she was too crushed to want to talk to anyone. On this day her gray situation had taken on a darker shade.

Because the weather was bleak, not many people were airing themselves. Nearly all of the benches were empty. Yet, deep within her thoughts, she walked as far as the duck pond in quest of an isolation that was all around her. Sitting down at last, what life she saw except for an occasional passer-by was in a scattering of pigeons and in a bedraggled squirrel combing the winter grass for food. Even the ducks had retired to some secret shelter. She wished that she could do the same.

Until recently, Addie Prentice's life had been woven of a pleasant homespun fabric. She had asked for nothing more than its simple pattern of keeping house, catering to family, and entertaining or being entertained by friends. She had never questioned the fabric's durability, and the great rent left by her husband's death had been a shock. But worse than that, it had left her exposed to elements she never knew existed.

She had rallied from the shock. She missed her husband, but she would have gone on much as before if she had remained in Gresham, South Carolina. Unfortunately, George Prentice, a lavish easygoing man, had saved little, and his insurance, taken out in the early days of marriage, had not kept pace with the rising costs of maintenance. He had always protected his wife's femininity from any coarse knowledge of finance, but she was a courageous woman and she did not fret about what could not be mended. She did not even blame him in her thoughts when she discovered that an unwise investment had swallowed up his printing business, leaving her only the heavily mortgaged house.

As soon as her initial grief and dismay subsided she prepared to make the best of things. She forwarded George's token legacies on to the children, sold the house, and made ready to become a boarder at a respectable establishment for paying guests. It would be, she realized, a change from her previous mode of existence, but she did not expect to find it untenable. She had been born and bred in Gresham to the age of sixty-seven. Friends and familiar scenery would still surround her. And unless she lived to an unreasonable old age, the money she had would see her through.

It did not occur to her to inform her son or her daughter of the state of her affairs. Since both had agreed that the house was too big for her and neither had expressed any desire to keep it in the family, she did not want to worry them with the fact that selling it was a matter of necessity rather than option. Moreover, to mention that George had not provided seemed a betrayal of his memory.

Her daughter, Nanny Lou, lived abroad with her husband who worked for an oil company. Nanny Lou had written a letter that was equivalent to a bucket of healing tears; sincerely mourning her father, sincerely regretful that her Tom's roving assignments did not permit her to offer her mother a home. This was to be expected in view of Nanny Lou's outgoing nature. It was the letter from Lindsey that struck a surprising chord.

Lindsey, her son, had settled in New York with his Northern wife. He had been teaching art in a high school there and had recently become an art supervisor. Addie Prentice had been deeply touched when he asked her to make a home with him. The brief note of invitation did not seem grudging to her. Lindsey was far from demonstrative and he had seldom used two words where one would do. Nor did his wife's carelessly scrawled postscript offend his mother's sense of decorum. She had simply thought, They want me. That's nice. And because she was an undemanding woman, a humble gratitude visited her.

Lindsey had been unable to take time off from his classes to attend his father's funeral. His rigid schedule had also prevented him from bringing his fiancée to South Carolina before the marriage. Addie's acquaintance with Elaine was therefore slight. She and George had traveled to New York for the wedding, but during the attendant activities there had been little chance to draw close to the girl. She had neither liked nor disliked her. Her predominant feeling at the time had been astonishment that anyone so poised and polished could be attracted to a son of hers.

After Lindsey's letter came, she thought that Elaine's cool exterior must contain an exceedingly warm heart, and she looked forward to knowing her better. Lindsey had said that he would not take "no" for an answer. But it required no masterful dictum to make her accept his generous offer. He was her flesh and blood. It was only natural that given a choice she should spend her remaining years with him. So she pulled up the few stakes that still held her to Gresham and set forth with every intention of adapting to and enjoying her new life.

Now, seated alone on the park bench near the pond, Addie Prentice tried once again to find the answers to the puzzling questions that had become her constant preoccupation. Why had Lindsey insisted upon bringing her to a home that was no home at all? And why had Elaine consented to an arrangement that was, at best, a matter of sufferance to her?

Not quite three months ago Elaine had met her at the station and taken her to the apartment hotel on West Fifty-eighth Street. Elaine had allowed her to pay for the cab, saying lightly that what with one thing and another a teacher's salary did not stretch very far. Elaine had ushered her to a small room, apologizing in a roundabout fashion for its shabbiness by stating that furnished rentals in New York were sky-high even in the lesser hotels and that this was the best they could do. Addie's innocent reply that she could have supplied furniture if she had realized the situation met with a peculiarly appraising look. Then Elaine had mentioned an important engagement, murmured something about food in the icebox, and departed to go about her business. It had seemed a casual sort of welcome, but Addie had refused to be disquieted by it. Later, she was forced to accord it significance.

Lindsey and Elaine were never guilty of overt rudeness to her. They merely boxed her off in a separate compartment from which she was unable to communicate with them. Lindsey performed the ritual of kissing her cheek each morning and asking how she fared. But he did not listen to her responses. He left them hanging in the air as though they were too unimportant to be gathered in, and he rejected the attempts she made at general conversation with flat monosyllables that would have given pause to the most insensitive of creatures. Addie's hide was neither thick nor thin. She was a normal woman with a normal will to be an active member of her milieu. Robbed of this right she pined.

She could not work off her frustrate longings by doing the housework or by cooking or shopping or by any of the tasks with which women of her upbringing filled their days. The hotel's cleaning staff serviced the apartment. The groceries were usually ordered by telephone. There was room for only one in the minute kitchenette, and Elaine insisted upon being that one, refusing all her wistful offers of assistance. And so, within a very brief span, she began to feel that her usefulness in any area of human performance was ended. How could it be otherwise since neither her son nor her daughter-in-law appeared to want what she might have contributed, either as companion or as eager slavey.

Most unbearable of all was the way they stopped talking the moment she entered a room. They had much to say to each other, she knew. The walls of the apartment were thin. At night in her bed she would lie awake, her thoughts entangled in the endless ribbon of words that went from one to the other. They were cautious. They tried not to speak above a murmur. But sometimes the ribbon stretched taut, and sometimes it tore with an ugly rending sound. She was no eavesdropper. She could not and did not try to grasp the meaning of what they said. Whenever their voices rose she muffled them by pulling the covers over her head. But "money" was the loudest and most frequent of their utterances, and she could not fend off its repeated onslaught upon her ears.

She gathered, of course, that they were having a difficult time in making ends meet, and she wanted very much to help. She would have offered to pay board, but she feared to offend Lindsey's pride. She decided upon another way, and on his birthday she presented him with a check for five hundred dollars. He looked at it, thanked her, and placed it in his wallet. His acceptance reminded her of something. One Christmas when he had been no more than six he had wanted a bicycle. Nanny Lou, a year and a half older, had received one, but Nanny Lou was sensible and could be trusted not to take risks. Both she and George had thought Lindsey too young for the hazards of a two-wheeler and they had given him a pedal-driven wagon instead. He had thanked them, but no adult could have conveyed more subtly that the wagon was as nothing in relation to his needs. It was the same with the check. Disappointed and hurt, she had told herself that she was being fanciful. Five hundred dollars was a considerable chunk out of her total assets. Even if Lindsey did not realize that, it was by any standards a generous birthday gift. And with it had gone the unacknowledged hope that it might buy her into his good graces since everything else had failed. But it did not engender even a temporary warmth. All was as before. Then suddenly it was worse.

At the beginning of her stay she had breakfasted with Lindsey. She was, by habit, an early riser, but in any case she would have made a point of spending a little time with him before he left for work. That was in the beginning. As time went by she had purposely dawdled in her room, her sore heart rebelling at his duty kiss, his perfunctory greeting.

This morning she had been standing quietly before the grudging mirror above the bureau. She had been brushing her soft white hair, slowly and painstakingly because she had nothing else to do. She had been listening for the closing of the outer door that would announce his departure. She wanted to go to the bathroom, to bathe so that she could dress. But she had reached the stage where she was loath to call attention to her undesired presence, and the apartment was so limited that its occupants could not help being conscious of each other's slightest move. This would have been no matter for concern if love lived there. But love was absent. Her dreary thoughts had gone on to a more practical consideration. Lindsey might want to use the bathroom before he left. So she waited.

Even with Lindsey gone there would be Elaine to face. But Elaine's indifference she could cope with and try to understand. Elaine was a bystander whose affection she had no right to expect. Elaine's involvement with her was neither biological nor by selection.

Except for the crackling of Lindsey's newspaper there was silence in the living room. If the two who sat over coffee thought of her at all, they must have thought she slept. If not they were past caring. Elaine spoke suddenly, making no effort to mute her clear voice. "I think you should tell her."

"Not again," Lindsey said. "We're not going over that again."

His mother could picture his dark handsome face, sullen and shut. "I can't tell her," he said. "We'll just have to do the best we can."

"The best we can is to send her back to Gresham. She'd be happier there."

Standing rooted, his mother thought she heard him say Nanny Lou's name. Then she thought she had imagined it out of her need for something dear and familiar in an alien world. She did hear him groan.

"Don't expect me to sympathize with you," Elaine said.

"What have I done that's so terrible?"

"I'm not blaming you for . . ." She lowered her voice and Addie missed the next few words. ". . . although you haven't even told me all the ins and outs of it, have you? But the thing is, I believed I was marrying a mature man——"

"Let me alone."

"I might at that."

"What are you talking about?"

"You understand me. I can't put up with it much longer. That's clear enough for you—isn't it?"

It was too clear, and undoubtedly Elaine had continued to speak clearly, but Addie Prentice heard no more. She forced her numbed limbs to obey her cringing mind. Animal stealth carried her back to bed, to the burrow of pillow and blanket that was proof against distinguishable words.

She did not hear Lindsey go. She did not hear Elaine tiptoe to the door or know that she looked in upon her. Dry-eyed, stiff with misery she lay, until instinct told her that she was alone in the apartment.

Later, when she arose and went through the motions of living, she was arrested every so often by a flicker of astonishment. For it seemed strange that she could still function as Addie Prentice, a respected member of society, now that she had become Addie Prentice, outcast.

Elaine had left a note for her. The scrawled words were reminiscent of the postscript to Lindsey's letter. "It was late for you to be sleeping," Elaine had written, "but I didn't like to wake you. I hope you're feeling all right. If you should need a doctor, call the one in the hotel. He's not bad."

Seated on the park bench, Addie told herself that if ever her balance was restored she might come to read a kind of wry humor into that note. Her daughter-in-law had told Lindsey that she was leaving him. "I can't put up with it much longer," she had said, meaning that she could not put up with his mother. And on the heels of that ultimatum she had taken time out to be considerate of his mother's health.

It was not the sudden gusty breath of March that prompted Addie to huddle within her coat. Neither was the action due to the invasion of her privacy. Minutes passed before she noticed that someone shared her bench.

Only when the woman cleared her throat did Addie become aware of her presence. Schooled in the mores of a small town she recognized the throat-clearing as a prelude to speech and felt that she must acknowledge it or forever after carry the stigma of rudeness. Dutifully she said, "Good afternoon."

"Excuse me—I find nothing of good in it."

Except for its foreign flavor, the pronouncement might have

issued from Addie's own depths. She turned to make appraisal of its source. Then she said, "Why—I've seen you before. You live on the same floor as I do—at the Hotel Vauban."

"Yes—I am pleased you notice."

Her expectant look put Addie under further obligation. She said lamely, "Why wouldn't I? We're neighbors."

"Neighbors? Ah—but here is a word that does not belong in New York City." The woman had a husky, not unpleasant voice. "We live in the same building—true. Even on the same floor. We travel together sometimes in the elevator going up or down. Yet we do not introduce—and when we step out we lose each the other. Is this being neighbors?"

Addie said, "Well—I guess not. At least not where I come from——" She added with a wealth of pride and longing, "Gresham, South Carolina."

"And not where I come from also," the woman said firmly. "A village in Hungary which I do not embarrass you by saying because it makes Americans to sneeze. This name you speak is in America, naturally."

"Of course," Addie said a little indignantly.

"Excuse. I ask in that you have a softer slower way than most I have met—except the dark-skinned peoples. And you are too pink and white to be of them."

Addie had to hunt for a reply. The best she could do was, "Oh." Then, for a moment, she lost herself in the reference that had been made to her complexion. Pink and white? Before leaving the apartment, she had glimpsed a set of blanched chill features which she hardly recognized.

Her companion said, "We are undoubtedly of an age—yes?"

The habit of politeness forced Addie to pull herself together. She said gallantly, "I'm sure you must be younger." Her eyes took in the gaily feathered hat worn with considerable style, the fine strong boning of face and body. In turn she realized that entry was being made of her own person, of neat plain attire encasing a no-nonsense plumpness.

"Perhaps," the woman said, "it is merely that I dress behind my years. I will arrive at sixty-eight on next my birth date."

"Why—so will I." Addie was inordinately pleased. She listened to the cheerful note in her voice as to an echo from the past. "But you've scarcely a line in your face."

"I agree," the woman said. "My image is to wonder at each time I look in my glass. My soul is a different matter. My soul is wrinkled like unfastened stockings."

She spoke with such dramatic relish that Addie could not help smiling. "I guess we all have our troubles," she said, and at once the smile faded. To her there was nothing banal in the words.

The woman's appreciative nod might have crowned the birth of an epigram. "I could not myself have expressed it better." There was a jauntiness even in her gloom. "And now it is time for us to introduce. I am Mrs. Sandor Barsony. If this makes your mouth too full my little name is Kate."

"It's a real pleasure to meet you, Mrs. Barsony. I'm Mrs. Prentice." Not to be outdone she supplied her own first name. "Addie Prentice."

"Prentice I am already acquainted with—in your son."

"My—you've met my son?"

"Oh yes. Also I have met your daughter-in-the-law. They visited with us before you came—but not since. A pity—no? For if they had continued we are introduced long ago."

A pity, Addie thought dully. She had been too preoccupied to wonder at their lack of friends. Only two people had called since her arrival—that Watling couple with whom they seemed to have little in common although the man was well educated. She moved uneasily. There had been plenty of young folks at the wedding. Must she, in addition to everything else, face the fact that they had curtailed their social life because of her? Were they ashamed of her, afraid that she would disgrace them? They never entertained or seemed to visit. On the rare occasions when they went out together they announced that it was to take in a movie. From the outset she had been robbed of her facility for putting normal curiosity into words. She had never questioned their circumscribed existence, and dignity had not even allowed her to speculate upon the solo comings and goings that absented Elaine for hours on end. And I won't speculate now, she thought. If Elaine is using me as an excuse to leave I'll give her no reason to substantiate it, not even an intangible reason. Unconsciously she held her head high. As for their being ashamed of me—why that's sheer nonsense. I got along all right in Gresham. People sought me out. I was—I was almost popular.

"Your son does not resemble you," Mrs. Barsony said.

"No—he's like George—my husband." She was impelled to amend it. "Physically—I mean." In no other way did he show a likeness to George. Dearest George.

"Your husband then is a very handsome man. You are not together with him in this city?"

"No." Addie did not want to amend that, but what she might have termed impertinence in anyone else seemed in Mrs. Kate Barsony the forthrightness of a child seeking common ground with a new friend. She could not administer a snub. "I'm a widow."

"Ha," said Mrs. Barsony. "Ha," she repeated. Her bright brown eyes gleamed with excitement. She raised slim gloved hands. She used the fingers of the left as a kind of abacus, her calculations starting with the thumb. "One—we occupy the same floor. Two—we meet in the elevator. Three—we make solitary excursions to the park to seek air. Four—we are widows both. Five—we are granted the roof of our married children—you by your son—I by my daughter. For all this is only one word." She pronounced it with bloodcurdling melodrama. "Destiny."

# 2

Addie experienced the inevitable reaction of sanity toward any deviation from the norm. She controlled her instinctive recoil and managed to say temperately, "It certainly is a coincidence—though I wouldn't be surprised if there were a gracious plenty of widows living in New York with their children."

"You call this living?" Mrs. Barsony's tone was bitter and knowing. Somehow it denied the implication of madness. So did the hands, now resting neat and quiet in her lap.

Reassured, Addie said, "I suppose it's not always too easy for the children either."

"Who speaks of always?" The hands came alive again. Mrs. Barsony waved an emphasizing finger under her companion's nose. "Who speaks of comical-book mothers who make trouble by pushing their two-centses into the business of their young? You are this type?"

"I hope not," Addie said. She thought of how she had bent

backward to keep from interfering with the affairs of Lindsey and Elaine.

"There! So it is not of 'always' we speak. It is of particular—of now—of us. We are human beings before we are mothers—no? And have we read it in any literature that being mothers makes for being less human? The years change our looks a little for the worse—our brains a little for the better is my opinion. But this makes the only difference in how we are today and how we are at the age of our children. Yet sometimes when they look on us we become no more than wooden furniture. No—do not tell me it is not the same with you for I will not believe. I have sensed our affinity in your face the minute we cross paths in the elevator—long before I follow you to this bench where no happy woman would sit on such a cold and stingy day——"

"You followed me?"

Mrs. Barsony nodded, her face unblushing. "Yes. So you see—it is not what you call coincidence. It is only that I give destiny a hurry-up. Naturally I follow you. Is there not a saying that misery loves company? Excuse if I speak too firm—but it is no use denying me you are miserable."

Addie tried to withstand the assault upon her code of what was fitting and what was not. The code definitely precluded complaining about her kin to a stranger in the park. She said, "I don't want you to get any wrong notions, Mrs. Barsony. My son, Lindsey, wouldn't have it any other way but that I come to live with him when my husband passed on. My son is——" She hesitated because she did not really know what her son was. Then she said defiantly, "He's a good boy."

Mrs. Barsony's eyes were pitying. "And my daughter, Jancsi, I suppose also to be a good girl." Fascinated, Addie saw that the third and fourth fingers of both gloved hands were crossed. Uncrossing them, Mrs. Barsony gathered volume. "As for my son-in-the-law—I do not at all suppose the same." She leaned toward Addie. "To me he is like nothing so much as this small animal with the big smell. I am not well acquainted with this animal and therefore the name of it escapes me."

Addie said with mechanical helpfulness, "A skunk?"

"Ah yes—you pick it right from my lips. My son-in-the-law is a skunk." She pronounced it, "Skoonk."

Addie burst out laughing. She laughed so hard that she had to take a handkerchief from her bag and dab at her streaming eyes. Gasping, she apologized. "I'm sorry—I don't know why I'm—I'm laughing—it—it's silly of me—oh dear—I——"

"Please not to mention. I do not intend to say jokes—but naturally there is a joke in everything and I am enchanted that like myself you have humorousness—only do not laugh so strong or it will turn against you."

It had turned. Thoroughly ashamed, Addie Prentice tried valiantly to control her tears.

Mrs. Barsony waited until she succeeded. "Weeping is also not bad," she said encouragingly. "For me it is unfortunate that I am a dry one who cannot ease myself in this way. Instead I choke inside where is more damage done than can be fixed with—for example—a powdering puff."

Addie responded to the delicate suggestion. She took out her compact and made repairs. A very old man shuffled past the bench and gave her a disapproving look. She thought with disbelief, Here I am making up in public like a chippy. But she did not care. Mrs. Barsony or the tears or both had made her feel better.

After a few moments of companionable silence, she said reluctantly, "I'm afraid I'll have to be going now, Mrs. Barsony. It's getting real chilly." She added mendaciously, "Besides—if I stay out too long my—they might worry."

"This kind of worry will do them good," Mrs. Barsony said. She seemed to have welded Addie's problem and her own into one lump. She got to her feet when Addie did. She was much the taller of the two, a slim and elegant figure wearing slightly outmoded clothes with such flair that they might have been the fashion of tomorrow. "We go in the same direction, no? So why not we go assembled?"

"That will be nice," Addie said.

"We make it yet nicer. We stop in at the Vienna Shop and we drink hot coffee with whipped cream to it. I treat."

"Why—you're very kind but I couldn't dream of letting you——"

Mrs. Barsony said regally, "A little matter. Next time perhaps is your turn."

"Well—all right." Addie thought sadly of the house in Gresham where neighbors might drop in for refreshment at any time of the day, and no one to gainsay their right to be there. How much she had taken for granted. How pleasant it would be to entertain Mrs. Barsony——

Mrs. Barsony seemed to read her thoughts. "With an establishment to call my own," she said, "I would propose a different invitation. You and I would sit over coffee in private—eating what my own cook has baked. But we will not waste time in bemoanings. Second to best is more than nothing at all."

On the way out of the park, the two ladies indulged in small talk. When Mrs. Barsony commented upon the bared bones of the trees, Addie said it was hard to believe that spring would soon be here and went on to say that in Gresham folks would be starting to plan their gardens. Opposite the Plaza, when Mrs. Barsony clicked her teeth in sympathy for an ancient coachman who sat with collar raised against the wind, Addie wondered aloud if he could possibly be the one who had driven her and George through the park on their first visit to New York. Then she and Mrs. Barsony looked at each other and sighed and followed their own memories back through the years.

The Vienna Shop was a block away from the hotel. Addie had peered into its windows often, her mouth watering at the display of pastries. But Elaine was either dieting or did not like sweets, and to introduce them to the somewhat sparse menu would have been in the nature of a tactless comment. Lindsey, as a child, had loved all manner of sweets. He had never seemed to get enough. Did he get enough now—of anything? Was he even to be robbed of what he had—of Elaine——?

She forced her thoughts to surface. She shook the slimy water from them and followed Mrs. Barsony into the Vienna Shop. She admired the assurance expressed by her erect carriage, her confident march down the cheerful humming room. She was surprised to see that in addition to non-alcoholic beverages the restaurant offered the fruits of a small glistening bar.

Mrs. Barsony turned and said with scorn, "Champagne on occasions yes—but the cocktails I drink never."

They sat down at one of the few unoccupied tables. Coffee arrived under heavy caps of cream. Earnest and deliberate consultation went into the selection of pastries from a large tantalizing assortment. Before the repast was over, Mrs. Barsony had become Kate, and Kate had made time fly by unburdening herself to her dear friend, Addie.

"It commences," Kate said, "with the barrenness of my sister who has married in America. You understand, Addie, that at the time I speak I am in Hungary with my beloved Sandor and my little Paul, and my Jancsi, and my Anna, and my Laszlo, who is just begun in me."

"Imagine!" Addie said. "Four children—and a figure like a girl's."

Kate shrugged. "Why not? I ride—I walk—I have throughout my days the healthy uncooped-up existence. Another time I will relate all about our beautiful estate. Now it is more important that I tell of my sister, who is childless no matter how she and her poor husband exert themselves. My sister and I remain close by letter writing and by visits that Sandor and I make to this country. Each time we come we bring our little ones in turn—and when it is Jancsi's turn my sister falls in love with her and cannot bear to part. Jancsi is five then—and how exquisite—and how wrong that Sandor names her for a boy—after his best friend. My sister begs to borrow her and Sandor and I have not the heart in us to refuse—especially with little Laszlo in the making and with Jancsi screeching like a fiend to stay with the aunt who spoils her. At first the arrangement is temporary—a short visit. But gradually it progresses to permanence. I do not wear you out with the many reasons for this. In chief, whenever we wish to recall Jancsi, my sister, who is delicate, sickens, so that it becomes brutality to deprive her. And that is how Jancsi happens to be brought up an American girl. Will you have another pastry, Addie?"

"Why—yes—I believe I will."

"I, too."

"Please go on about Jancsi." Genuine interest had spread a salve over Addie's troubles. Somewhere under that salve the wounds of the morning lay ready to throb again. But for the moment they slept.

"You find the story fascinating, yes? Very well—I go on. Sandor and I continue to make many trips forth and back. Money is nothing in those times. Everyone has it—Sandor—I—my sister—you perhaps?"

Addie nodded.

"I thought so. You have the look." At Addie's skeptical expression, she said, "This look has not to do with jewels and minks. It is more basical. Where have I been? Oh yes—naturally today money is another horse entirely. Even before Sandor dies we are sick in the pocketbook—although I do not soon realize to what big extent."

Addie said, "That's the way it was with me. I never really understood just how we were fixed until George passed away."

"You see?" Kate Barsony accepted this as further proof that their lives had run along parallel lines. She chewed cake ruminatively. "With Sandor gone—and all things else marching backwards," she said, "I become at my string's end and do not know what to do. I am now in England—for I have taken my Paul and my Anna by the hand and crept from under the Iron Curtain. In England my children fall into love and marry and are content—although between them they have few coins to rattle. As for my brave young Laszlo—he has been shot by a Russian——" She choked on the words. "Excuse please—a crumb has strayed to the pipes——"

Addie excused, realizing sympathetically that the brief coughing spell covered grief.

"Well—I make short of the story. The estate has melted until it does not any more exist—and when Jancsi invites me to America where she has transformed to a citizen I sell a few things here and there to collect my passage—pack up my remainders—and make yet another sailing. I am under the impression you understand that Jancsi can well afford an extra mouth. My poor sister and my brother-in-the-law are gone—but they leave her a little fortune. Also she has married and always she writes that she and her man are prospering. But what I find when I arrive is different. The only way her man prospers is by marriage to her money. If he has another occupation I am unable to place my finger upon the nature of it." She spread her hands to pantomime nothingness. "So here we are," she said, "and the feast is done."

Addie understood that she was not referring to the emptied plates and cups. She said sadly, "There doesn't seem much that we can do about it."

"I am not defeated. It may be that with two heads to put together we will find means to remedy our situation." Suddenly she giggled. It was a very young sound. "In the days when your daughter-in-the-law came with your son to visit I have remarked upon her beauty."

The non sequitur bewildered Addie. Her brow wrinkled.

"My son-in-the-law is also considered to be handsome," Kate Barsony said. "Not by me—but by some." Her bright eyes narrowed mischievously. "I do not exactly say they are birds of a feather—but I present you with the idea that we attract them to each other's attention." She shrugged. "Who knows what might result of it?"

Addie was shocked. It took her a moment to grasp that her companion was jesting. Then she laughed uncertainly.

"You do not think I am wicked? Good."

It was nonsense, but it was diverting nonsense. Daringly Addie made her contribution. "If they were on visiting terms and nothing happened I'm afraid we'll have to think of something else." But it was not really a joke and she could not continue to treat it as one. She said soberly, "I—I'm sort of playing with the notion of going back to Gresham but——"

"I think of Europe too—although where to raise the fare is for me a larger business than for you."

"It isn't the fare so much—it's——"

"I know. It is first to jump over the awkwardness of explaining to your son that you are not content with him—and then it is the losing of your face in brazening to your home people why you return hanging the tail—no?"

"Yes," said Addie. She did not explain that it was more than that. If put to it, she thought, she could weather the avid curiosity of old friends and neighbors. But could she live on what was left of her resources, drained by paying the grocer boy and the cleaner who more often than not arrived when Lindsey and Elaine were out, drained by her gift to Lindsey, drained by numerous small items of which she had lost track. I'll manage somehow, she thought, as though unknown to her the decision had taken definite shape. I've still a good round sum. I'll eke it out by baby-sitting or find other odd jobs. I'll manage.

"I also take no pleasure in hanging the tail," Mrs. Barsony said, "and therefore it is not the right answer." Her small hand struck the neat region of her breast. "But how I am selfish. When I join you on the bench I see you bundled up in a despair that is far thicker than mine since I am not by habit the despairing kind. Yet, what do I do? I speak so much of Kate Barsony that you have no chance to unbundle. Do so now. I give you all my ears."

Addie could not do so. The salve had melted. The wounds throbbed again, and the throbs fused into that amorphous pain called forth by the conversation she had overheard.

She looked down at the little wrist watch that had been an anniversary present from George. "Heavens!" she said. "I really must be going. It is almost six. They will be——" What would they be? She could not finish it.

Walking the darkening streets, there was little small talk. Kate Barsony was unresponsive, and Addie too became silent before they reached the dirty gray building that was the Hotel Vauban. Mixed with her dominant anxiety was the hope that her failure to return confidence for confidence had not offended.

Her artificially bolstered spirits continued to drop with the ascent of the old-fashioned elevator. Her parting, "Thank you for the delicious treat," was graciously if absently received. It was even followed by an assurance of further meetings. Yet she felt completely deserted as Kate Barsony's door closed behind her, and she had to make several tries before her own key would mate with the lock of Lindsey's and Elaine's apartment.

Her little bedroom opened off the small square foyer. She went straight to it. As she removed her hat and coat she could hear activity in the kitchenette. There was no sound to indicate

Lindsey's presence. He might be poring over student offerings in the living room, although lately he had not been doing that. She suspected that in this too she was to blame, that just having her around was a distraction that prevented concentration. Certainly he no longer came straight home from school, which must mean that he stayed after hours to do the required work.

Well, if he was at home, or when he came home, she was going to talk to him. No matter what he was doing, no matter how impatient he looked, she would pin him down. She would find out exactly where she stood, and why. She smiled in forlorn tribute to Kate Barsony. Much better that she return to Gresham "with the tail hanging," than disrupt her son's whole life.

Lindsey was not in the living room. She sat down weakly. She hoped that he would come soon. It was going to be difficult to keep her resolution at the right heat. Then he walked out of the kitchenette and she was so surprised to see him that she could say nothing at all.

He said, "I heard you come in. I thought you were Elaine."

"I thought *you* were."

"She hasn't come in yet. I only just got in myself. I was having a glass of milk."

It was after six, and the mother in her mourned that there should be no hot meal waiting for him, nor even the fragrant promise of a meal. She said timidly, "I could fix dinner if——"

"No—she'll be here soon."

Would she? The words of the morning might have been a dream for all the concern he showed. He sat down, opened a magazine, and idly turned its pages. He was in his shirt sleeves, and his shirt did not look too clean. Under an incipient beard his face had the gray patina of fatigue.

"Lindsey," she said. She expected, as she had been led to expect, that he would say, "Well?" without troubling to raise his eyes. But he laid the magazine aside and looked full at her.

He said, "Mother—I've been wanting to talk to you. I guess this is as good a time as any. The fact is——" Suddenly he looked vulnerable. He looked like the disarming boy who went unpunished because George could not bear to discipline him.

She said, "Lindsey—if it's about my living here I realize it hasn't worked out. I know you had the best of intentions but there's no real harm done. I can go back to Gresham——"

"Mother—hold on—you've got it wrong——"

"You needn't try to soften it. There won't be any hard feelings——"

He got out of his chair, a big man physically, both tall and broad. He came toward her, almost, she thought unbelievingly, as though he intended to put his arms around her. Through wonder she heard the knocking at the door.

Lindsey's advance stopped. He said, "Damn—Elaine must have forgotten her key. I'll go."

Addie stood up, dazed at what had surely been the start of recognition long withheld. It took several moments for her to realize that he was talking to someone at the door, and that the someone was not Elaine.

She heard him say, "I've told you—my mother's busy. I'm sorry——" He did not sound sorry. He sounded rude and harsh.

She went out to the foyer. Mrs. Barsony was there. Mrs. Barsony wore a frightened face. She seemed to have shrunk since afternoon. When she saw Addie she said urgently, "My friend—you must please come. There is trouble in my house."

"We don't want to be involved in your troubles," Lindsey said.

His mother squeezed past the barrier he made. "Forgive my son," she said. "Of course I'll come."

# 3

The apartment was different in layout. It had a long hall instead of a small square foyer. Down this Kate Barsony hurried, followed by Addie. Neither of the two ladies noticed that Lindsey dogged their steps.

There were doors on either side of the hall. Kate Barsony grasped a knob and turned it. She beckoned Addie across the threshold.

Almost piece for piece the room's furniture matched that of the Prentice master bedroom. But Lindsey and Elaine were tidy people, and obviously those who shared this room were not. Disorder lent a kind of warmth to the hotel stereotype. A miscellany of garments had been thrown over chairs. Masculine and feminine toilet aids battled for priority on bureau and dressing table. And a vital perfume hung in the air contributing to the general atmosphere of clutter.

Atop the crumpled spread on one of the beds lay a man. He did not move. Addie's heart lost a beat and then pumped overtime in compensation. So unhoped for was his groan.

Kate Barsony said with ludicrous formality, "Mr. Joe Montheil—my son-in-law." And at the sound of her voice the groan took on a definite note of protest. She went on aloofly, "Perhaps assistance is not needed after all. I think he strengthens."

Addie approached the bed. She saw a slight figure fully clothed. She saw a bloodied face so battered that it was hard to determine the original cast of the features. She said, "What's happened to him?" and because she hated violence, the words sounded angry and accusing.

Kate Barsony shrugged helplessly. "He does not say. I enter the apartment. I start down the hall believing I am alone. I hear this sudden noise he makes—rush in and find him. He hides his face—so I make a sniff and I—I think what I think."

Addie sniffed too. Now that she was beside the bed she could smell the fumes of liquor.

"My Jancsi is not at home and me he will not let near although I have made ready to do my duty." Kate indicated the bureau. Amid the confusion was a basin of water, a box of absorbent cotton, and an iodine bottle. "Disinfection he needs I know. What else is to judge by feeling him."

Joe Montheil's eyes did not open, but he parted his lips. One gutter syllable emerged.

Addie said, "I'm afraid he needs more than nursing." She heard a snort of laughter and became aware of Lindsey in the doorway. His face was humorless, denying the laugh. "Lindsey—you get that doctor up here—the one in the hotel that Elaine——" She stopped, overwhelmed by the impression that she called to him from a distance too vast for hope of audibility. This was confirmed by his unresponsive stance.

Her attention was drawn back to the bed. Slowly Joe Montheil had attained to sitting posture. What effort it cost him was manifested by sweat. It weighted locks of dank fair hair to his brow and diluted the blood upon his cheeks. Addie leaned over and curved an arm around his shoulders. She said, "Don't try to move—just lie back——"

He opened one eye. It focused upon her and she felt glued to its blue iris. Then the other eye opened and the effect of that awful wink was dispelled. She bent close to glean the words from his swollen mouth.

"No doctor," he said thickly. "Get it—no doctor."

"This tune he also sings to me," Kate Barsony said defensively.

"But he's probably in so much pain he doesn't know what he's saying. You should have called one anyway."

"None is recorded in the addresses book—and my stupid wits fail to remind that a doctor stops in this hotel."

"Well—if you'll show me where your phone is——"

Joe Montheil leaned heavily against her supporting arm. She could not remove it. He said, "No doctor—savvy? Or are you another hunky?" The labored mumble in no way impaired his insolent intent.

"What——?"

"Skip it. I want a drink."

"Is understood a drink for him means only spirits," Kate Barsony said. She left the room.

He muttered something that sounded like, "She'll poison me," but because of his impaired speech Addie could not be sure. He refused to obey her command to lie down, so she continued to support him. And all the while Lindsey stood in the doorway saying and doing nothing.

Kate Barsony returned with a glass, which she passed to Addie. "I find the bottle outside the cabinet," she said. "He has already consulted it."

The hand he reached out for the glass was shaking, but he managed to toss a generous measure of its contents past his puffy vulnerable lips. He gulped several times and grunted loudly in pleasure or pain.

Kate Barsony said to no one in particular, "Should I be desired I am inside." She gave Addie a meaningful glance and the next moment was gone. Addie was so at loss to interpret the glance that she thought she had imagined it.

She addressed her patient. "Now you'll feel better."

"Sure." His speech had cleared a little. "Next stop the wheel chair and the tin cup."

"Where does it hurt?" She spoke as to a fractious child.

"Stick around while I draw up a catalogue."

"Why are you so silly about having a doctor?"

"One bit me when I was a lad. Why didn't the old witch bring the bottle?"

"Shame!"

He tried to smile. "Where did she find *you?*"

"I'm Mrs. Prentice—Lindsey's mother."

His eyes shifted toward the door where Lindsey stood. He said carefully, "Impossible. That phony son of a——"

He pushed against her arm with such force that she had to remove it. He fell back, shielding his battered face with his arms, and she saw that Lindsey was advancing upon him. He moaned, "He'll finish me——"

"Lindsey!" But the authority in her voice was wasted. Lindsey had halted of his own accord. He reversed himself. The floor boards shook as he quit the room, slamming the door behind him.

"All right," Addie said. "He's gone."

Cautiously, Joe Montheil lowered his arms. He muttered, "Real gone—and that's not hep talk."

She did not understand the sense of what he said. The tone she recognized. "You behave—hear?" She cleared a chair for the basin of water. She sponged his face. He winced and swore a little as she applied the iodine. But he did not resist. The damage appeared less frightening with the blood washed away. Next she fingered the scalp under his thick fair hair. She found no lump or open wound.

"Does it ache?"

"No more than the rest of me."

"Can you take off your jacket?"

"Lady—there's a time and place for everything."

She set her mouth sternly, and in pretended abashment he said, "I only meant I should have taken it off before I was jumped."

"I don't care one bit what you meant. All I know is you can't be too hard off—the way you talk."

He co-operated while she removed the jacket and unbuttoned his shirt. Against his fair white skin red welts and livid bruises stood out in sharp relief. But so far as she could determine there were no broken bones.

"How do your legs feel?" she asked.

He moved them experimentally. "They work."

"I still think it's plain foolish not to have a doctor. I took a first-aid course but——"

"Listen—you-all—even Southern-type witches understand English if they try real hard. No doctor."

She straightened her plump little body. "I'm inclined to be sorry for anyone who's had a good licking—but it appears to me from the way you go on that you deserved it."

This time his smile was more successful. For a fleeting moment the battered features were overlaid by a kind of poisonous sweetness. Or so it seemed to her.

Disturbed, she said, "Well—there's nothing more I can do. I'll be going now."

"Where?" It was abrupt and demanding.

"Watch your manners," she said stoutly. "You be polite if you want me to answer questions. I'm going home—not that it's any worry of yours."

He raised himself again. Again the sweat crawled from under his hairline. "It might be—if you've any idea of mentioning this to the police."

It had not crossed her mind. Her candid face told him so. He changed the subject to correct a tactical error. "Ouch—I got a cut on the inside of my mouth."

"Open wide—let me see."

"I can't. My jaw feels muscle-bound."

"I don't notice it interfering with your talk any," she said. Relenting, she removed the basin from the bedside chair, sat down, and swabbed the sweat from his brow and cheeks. "In my opinion there's nothing much wrong except you're weak as a kitten—and no wonder."

He leaned against the softness of her arm. He muttered, "Stick around."

"Hush. Lie down again. Long as there's nothing broken the best cure for you is sleep."

"I don't want to sleep. I like it this way."

It seemed to her that he stayed "this way" for ages. She began to wonder at and to resent the prolonged absence of Kate Barsony. After all, there were limits even to being a good neighbor. And come to think of it, where was his wife? What was there about the big city that bred women so derelict in their duty that they were not around when their men needed them? She grew very tired, but his back felt thin and boyish against her arm, and it had been so long since anyone had wanted her support. He was not a nice young man, she thought. Yet—— "Would you like me to help you into your pajamas before I go?" she said gently. "You'd be much more comfortable."

"No—I'll die with my boots on."

She seized upon it as an excuse to move. "Well—bless my soul." She took her arm away. He lay back, meeting the bed gingerly, and she bent to remove his shoes.

"What now?" he said. "Do we play 'this little piggy'?"

"I should have taken your shoes off first thing. You'll rest better."

"Mammy—you're growing on me. If you were a newer model I'd trade my wife in for you."

"Where does your wife keep extra blankets?"

"I don't even know where the hell she's keeping herself."

Addie went to the closet. It was as untidy as the rest of the room. A pile of comic books toppled off a shelf, just missing her head. She replaced them. She found a blanket and covered him.

"That's the best I can do," she said, "unless you let me go the whole hog and put you to bed."

He looked up at her. "Lindsey's not your son."

"He certainly is."

"Don't get mad. That was a compliment."

"What have you got against Lindsey?"

"Brother! But one thing I'll give him—he knows his onions. Only you should have washed his mouth out with soap—no—I guess not his mouth—his hands——"

Her disdain was elaborate. "You're making a lot of sense."

"He makes less—after meeting you. You must have goofed——"

"Goofed?"

"Laid an egg——"

"Mr. Montheil—in all my born days I never heard——" She had an impulse to flounce from the room, but something held her. As though Lindsey still stood in the doorway she saw the rolled sleeves of his limp tieless shirt, the expenditure of physical energy implicit in his air of bodily weariness. Nothing about him suggested a man who had spent the day in sedentary occupation. She shook her head to dislodge the limpet-like suspicion. Lindsey was unmarked, and even a long drink of water like Montheil would have managed to inflict a bruise or a scratch in self-defense. Nevertheless, she said carefully, "Who gave you the licking?"

"It wasn't Superman."

"Never mind being so smart. There's no call to brag about being up on your comics."

"Huh?"

She laid a restraining hand on his shoulder to keep him from sitting up again. "A little bit ago you seemed scared the police would hear about this—and I wouldn't be surprised if Lindsey has told them."

"Him report anything to the police! Remind me to laugh when I've got my health."

"I don't see a thing to laugh at. If hoodlums can get into this hotel and beat the tenants the police should know so's they'll keep it from happening again."

"Who said anything about hoodlums? Maybe I just got into a friendly argument."

"Decent men find other ways to settle their differences."

"Decent? You've got quite a vocabulary, Mammy." Then he said, "Lindsey hasn't called the police—and you won't either."

"Why won't I?"

"Because if you do I'll tell them Lindsey did it."

He sounded drowsy, but she ignored her edict concerning sleep. "Did he?" she said.

"What's that got to do with it?" He yawned. It was a mistake. Tenderly he fingered the abused region of his mouth.

"Was it Lindsey?"

"Don't worry. I won't tattle." He closed his eyes. He said nothing more, but after a few moments had passed he did at least shatter the silence. She was inclined to doubt the authenticity of his almost too stertorous snoring.

Her voice was a challenge. "All right—I'm leaving now. I hope you'll be a better man when you wake." Tentatively, she started for the door. She was arrested, not by Joe Montheil but by voices in the hall.

Someone said in a throaty contralto, "I guess I can't keep you out of the apartment but I can keep you out of my bedroom." That was followed by crude male laughter and such sounds as might have been used in gentling a horse.

Addie was about to open the door that Lindsey had slammed and make her presence known, but the owner of the contralto cried in blistering anger, "You—you get out of here, Fix." Then the doorknob turned, and like a small tornado a girl whirled into the room.

Looking past her into the hall, Addie saw no one. She did, however, hear retreating footsteps, and was brushed by a passing thought that they sounded much too light to match her mental concept of the unseen villain.

Her admonishing hand brought the girl to a standstill. She stood poised on one foot, breathing hard. Addie's involuntary smile was the tribute exacted by her beauty. She said, "I think he's gone to sleep. Are you Jancsi?"

The girl nodded, looking completely bewildered. "Who are——?" She followed the turn of Addie's head. "Joe—what's happened to Joe?"

Addie was distressed. "Didn't your mother tell you?"

"She's not here. What——?" She started toward the bed. Addie intercepted her, wanting to soften the shock. "I think he looks worse than he is. But maybe you can coax him to have a doctor." She half expected the recumbent figure to sit up and repeat his ultimatum. He kept on snoring. If he was playing possum, she thought, he was certainly putting his heart and soul into it.

Indignation crossed Jancsi's triangular face. "He's snoring!" And as though the inanity of the statement struck her, she added lamely, "I mean—he never does." She by-passed Addie and went to the bed. She looked down. Her eyes, slightly upslanted in her face, widened. Her teeth caught and held the curve of her lower lip, and then let go. She showed no other sign of stress. She said, "Joe," several times, making of it a soft full-throated sound. And then she turned away.

Addie felt that what might have started out as a pretense was now a fact. She thought that no man awake could have failed to respond to his name uttered in such a way.

Jancsi said, "I don't understand. Did he tell you how——?"

"He didn't have to tell me. Anyone can see he's been in a fight. I live next door. Your mother called me in. I don't know where she could've got to." The last sentence contained a touch of acid.

"He didn't say who——?"

"No."

"Well—thank you very much for what you've done. I'll take over now."

She used the small prim utterance of one who is forced to exert supreme control to keep from breaking. Addie longed to hold her close and so encourage the release of tears. But that was a job for the girl's mother. And where on earth was——?

Kate Barsony burst into the room, gesturing over her shoulder at the little fat man who followed. "I bring the doctor from the hotel," she said breathlessly. "My regrets that I leave you alone holding the sack, Addie, but I could not get him by telephone so I have gone down to his office and waited all this while for the departure of his last client. Ah, Jancsi—you are home. You will now insist that your husband display his ills to this good man of medicines."

Something that was not a snore came from Joe Montheil. He sat up, face suffused, eyes popping. He gasped and sputtered in what sounded like choked rage. A mask of hatred and betrayal settled upon his distorted features. Then he sank back, renouncing the small assembly.

The doctor advanced at a waddling gait to the bedside chair.

He sat down. His short arm stretched out, and his fat fingers bared and made contact with Joe Montheil's wrist.

Watching, Addie saw his full small lips pucker as though he tasted bitter fruit. What he did by way of examination when he dropped the wrist seemed perfunctory, a task of rote.

# 4

The hotel doctor made his pronouncement much in the manner of one who has been victimized by practical jokers. "This man is dead," he said coldly, and his eyes darted from Addie to Jancsi to Kate Barsony as to three promising targets for his almost palpable mistrust.

Addie said, "But that's impossible," in a strange dry voice that broke bounds and rushed this way and that. "He just sat up—you saw—and he was talking to me—bold as you please. I attended to him the best I could and felt him all over to see if——" She stopped, distracted by Jancsi's hands gripping the footboard of the bed. She raised her eyes to Jancsi's face and thought that it was like a shriveled heart. There was no simile for Kate Barsony's face before compassion settled upon it and she turned to her daughter. Jancsi did not heed her outstretched arms. Jancsi continued to grip the bedpost and to stare at death.

"So you attended to him the best you could," the doctor said.

He seemed to take it for granted that Addie was a member of the household. "Well—he's been attended to all right. I wonder that you bothered to call me—but of course you wanted a death certificate. Sorry I can't oblige——"

His open rudeness gave Addie the brace she needed. She said hotly, "I can't imagine what you have in mind to use such an unprofessional tone. Why would we want a death certificate when we didn't even dream——?"

Kate Barsony spoke, tearing her eyes from Jancsi. "I also cannot imagine. I tell you from my own observances that he sits up—speaks—and is in everything except the appearance his usual. Therefore——?"

"Madame—you'll have ample opportunity to tell your story to the proper authorities." The doctor stood on his short legs, clutched his black bag, and waddled doorward. "I'm a busy man. I'll wait until the police come, of course, but the sooner I notify them——"

"The sooner you do not keep waiting these clients of yours from Park Avenue." Kate Barsony blocked his way.

His pudgy face reddened. "Madam—I don't pretend to be a fashionable practitioner——"

"You do not even pretend the politeness of your calling," Kate said. "With what cause do you behave so hinting? And why must these police of yours bring in their big feet? Do you turn over in your head that myself or my Jancsi or my heartful neighbor have made the fist against this recent Mr. Montheil?"

Again his eyes went from one to the other, but this time lingered long enough to see. He took in the fragile aging elegance of the woman who had summoned him, the respectable shape of Addie, and last, the frieze-like quality of the motionless girl. He said with somewhat more grace, "I'm not hinting at anything. I came up here expecting to treat a living patient. What has just occurred would have been all in the day's work —if natural causes were responsible. But it's obvious that he did not die of natural causes—which makes it a matter for the police."

"How did he die?" Addie said abruptly.

He shrugged. His eyes had returned to Jancsi. "Someone should get this girl to bed. I'll leave her a sedative."

"How did he die?" Addie repeated.

"My dear lady"—his patience was grudging—"I can't answer your question without further examination—which under the circumstances doesn't appear to be my job."

Jancsi wheeled upon them suddenly, her eyes blazing. "Will you stop! Will you have the decency to leave——"

"Yes," Kate Barsony said. "We must not stand here to make indelicate after-mortems. But you also, my poor little love, shall leave with us——"

The doctor laid his fat hand upon Jancsi's arm. "Your mother's right. No good being morbid. A warm bath and——"

She cowered away from him. "Mother—please—I'll stay with Joe——" It was a wild plea backed by a wild will. It drove them into the hall.

At the sound of the turning key in the closed door behind them, the doctor shook his head. But Kate Barsony said, "Do not for a moment concern yourself. Jancsi will commit no foolishness. She is after all my daughter and shortly will gather her senses together. Now call if you must your authorities."

So it was literally over Joe Montheil's dead body that the police were summoned. Addie started to leave before they made their appearance, but she was stayed by a complicacy of reasons. When the doctor said that the police would want to question her since she had been the last person to hear Joe Montheil speak, she did not point out that they could find her next door. She did not want to be found next door. It made no sense, she told herself, for Lindsey and Elaine to be dragged into the mess. Weakly, she built upon that. They would have real cause for annoyance at such an unnecessary intrusion of their privacy. And besides, what could she have been thinking about to desert Kate Barsony in her hour of need?

Later, it became patent to her that she rather than Kate needed aid and comfort. And again and again she found herself insisting silently that the sickness rising in the pit of her stomach was due to too much coffee and pastry, or it was the result of going dinnerless. Or else she had caught a chill in the park, or was suffering a reaction from the scene of the morning, or even more validly from the shock of having a young man die almost in her arms. In short, her malaise had its roots in anything but the sight of a disheveled Lindsey advancing upon Joe Montheil, who had cried out in terror, "He'll finish me." Finish!

It seemed to her that no time at all elapsed before the police arrived. It further seemed that they stayed for long enough to lop years from her life's expectancy.

The vanguard was formed by two plain-clothes detectives, reassuringly commonplace men such as might participate in give and take about the weather on any street in any town. They were followed by a medical examiner who routed Jancsi from the bedroom in short order and delivered her, not without kindness, into her mother's keeping. After the examiner came a small battery of technicians armed with the instruments of their special science.

No one made a dissenting motion when Kate Barsony vanished into her own bedroom with the benumbed Jancsi. The medical examiner engaged in a brief consultation with the hotel doctor, using terminology incomprehensible to a lay listener. The hotel doctor departed. The medical examiner and the detectives joined the technicians who had started upon their mysterious activities. Commanded to wait, Addie drifted into the living room.

Here, as in the bedroom, clutter prevailed, imparting surface warmth to the colorless furniture. On top of a bookshelf, empty save for tattered magazines, an elaborate silver coffee service sat in tarnished arrogance. A gate-legged table was almost covered with scattered playing cards, several of which had drifted to the threadbare rug. The locks of an old desk which seemed too fine a piece to have been provided by the management bore wanton scratches. A loudly patterned tie hung languidly over a chair back, and someone had dropped swatches of bright material upon the stiffly neutral couch. Filled ash trays were everywhere. It was as though the hotel maid had given up in despair.

Addie walked about. Absently she gathered the scattered playing cards and decked them. Absently she paused before a thick growth of pictures upon a papered wall. They were a hodgepodge of photographs and art reproductions, and one or two original oils, and they had been hung without taste or plan, apparently just as they had come to hand. A man's face caught her attention for a moment, because it looked familiar, but she was too distrait to attempt to place it. She moved to the couch, folded and laid aside the swatches, and sat down. She leaned against the ungiving upholstery and tried to tidy her thoughts. Somewhere a clock struck eight but she did not hear it. She wondered if Elaine had come home; if Lindsey had been fed. She wondered why one or the other of them had not seen fit to call her to dinner. Lindsey knew where she was. But of course she was where she was against his wishes. And of course he was unaware that her stay had not been lengthened out of choice. Of course he could not be aware of that.

Presently she was joined by the two detectives. They switched on lamps as they crossed the room. Even before they reached her they seemed to swallow the room's details in a series of great bites.

One of them addressed her. "Is this the way it always looks?"

"I don't know. It's the first time I've seen it."

Both stood and stared down at her. The clinical objectivity of their eyes at once metamorphosed their ordinary everyday appearance into something quite outside her ken. It made no difference that one detective was dark, the other sandy-haired, or that they were dissimilar in height and build. To Addie, because of their eyes, they became identical twins.

They took turns at questioning her, asking first her name and her connection with the Barsony-Montheil household. They listened closely to her story of how she had come to be in at the death. She told it with considered brevity, sitting composed and upright, with only a little too much precision in her speech to betray strain. When she had finished they took her through it again.

"You say you never met this Mrs. Barsony until today in the park?"

"I've seen her before—but today was the first time we spoke."

"Just like that?"

"Just like what? She shared my bench on purpose. She'd noticed me in the hotel and she felt it was time to get acquainted."

"Seeing you scarcely knew her—didn't it seem funny—her calling on you right away for help?"

"It didn't seem a bit funny. Sometimes it doesn't take long for people to know each other. Mrs. Barsony and I hit it off from the start. We found out we—we had a lot in common. And she probably couldn't think of anyone else to turn to in an emergency like that."

The sandy one glanced at his dark twin, who said, "An emergency like that is the kind most people would like to keep in the family—if you want to look at it as an emergency. According to you the death came as a complete surprise."

"It certainly did," Addie said.

"So it couldn't have seemed like an emergency in the beginning. How long have you been living in this hotel?"

"Two and a half months."

"And Mrs. Barsony?"

"I couldn't say—but probably a lot longer than that."

"Which means she could have made plenty of friends here—her not being too standoffish to talk to strangers in the park."

"Well," said Addie uncomfortably, "living right next door I reckon I was the handiest."

The sandy one took over. "You come from the South?"

Addie nodded, and said for the comfort of it, "Gresham, South Carolina."

"I've always heard that Southerners are pretty choosy. Yet in a couple of hours you're bosom pals with a foreign lady. If I remember right you said you had a lot in common with her."

"Why not? No matter where they're born people are people."

"Yeah," said the sandy one, obviously finding the statement no cause for elation. "Well—say your story's true——"

"Of course it's true."

"That's what I said." His voice was bland. "I'm only trying to get it straight in my mind. You met her in the park. On the way home you stopped for coffee and cakes. You parted on this floor, each going your own way. And how soon after that did she come knocking?"

"Ten minutes or so."

"Were you alone in your apartment?"

Addie took her time. "No—my son had come home. We were having a talk when——"

"I didn't hear you mention that before."

"Likely I forgot," Addie said calmly. "It didn't seem to have much to do with——"

"Your son let you come in here alone after Mrs. Barsony said there was trouble?"

"Oh no!" The exclamation rebuked him for thinking her son so careless of his mother's safety. "He came right along, too—but he didn't stay. He saw that there was nothing he could do. Mr. Montheil was sitting up and he said he didn't need a doctor so——"

"We'll come back to that. How long has your son lived here?"

"He and his wife moved in right after they were married. They've been married for a little more than two years."

"Sounds like they might be around the same age as the Montheils. Are they acquainted?"

Addie said, "If so they never mentioned it or had them to visit since I've moved in. Of course my son works real hard. He's a schoolteacher." She used a deprecating tone for Lindsey's occupation, somehow managing to invest it with spectacles and a frail stoop-shouldered physique. "Folks envy schoolteachers for having short hours—but even since he's become a supervisor I've seen him bring home a whole day's work—so it isn't as if he has much time left over for social life. He and Elaine go to the movies once in a while but mostly they sit home and chat or listen to the radio or——"

"We don't have much time for social life either." The dark one had broken in quickly, making it clear that he was practiced in dealing with the irrelevant disclosures of wandering witnesses. But Addie, for the moment at least, had achieved her purpose. He veered away from Lindsey. "Mrs. Prentice—you tell us it was a little after six when you came into the Montheils' bedroom. You must have been alone with Montheil for quite a while between the time that Mrs. Barsony sneaked out to get the doctor and the time she returned with him." He waited for her reluctant nod.

"Yes—I was alone with him until his wife came home."

"All right—so what I want is for you to concentrate on everything that was said and done within that period because you just might have skipped something that would finger the murderer."

She swallowed. "Murderer?" She could hardly get the word out.

Both detectives' eyes were upon her, suspiciously, she thought. "Well—manslaughter at any rate," the sandy one said.

"I don't think I left anything out," she said, and tried prayerfully to convince herself that failure to include the incident of Lindsey and Joe was an omission of no possible significance. "He talked mostly about not wanting a doctor. He asked for a drink and Mrs. Barsony brought it before she left. It revived him some." She had to fight off the sensation of a boyish back pressing against her arm. "He was real pert when I washed his face and tried to find out how bad he was hurt. I could see he was weak of course—he sweated a lot—and I wanted him to sleep. But he wouldn't—not at first. He just wouldn't lie down. And then at last he did—and I took off his shoes and covered him. As soon as he began to snore I thought it safe to leave. I was getting ready when his wife came—and you know what happened after that." She put a definite period to it.

Neither of the detectives showed satisfaction. The sandy one spoke. "He must have said *something* in all that time."

"He did and he didn't. I mean he was sort of fresh—not—not like a man fixing to die. He called me 'Mammy' and said too bad I wasn't younger. Nonsense like that."

"And not—for example—nonsense like who had beaten up on him?"

"No—though I did ask him. I thought maybe hoodlums had got into the hotel and if so the police should be told about it." She was talking too fast. She slowed, hoping that they had not noticed. "He wouldn't give me a yes or no about it being hoodlums. He said it could be he'd just got into a friendly argument." And now let me alone, she cried silently. Stop badgering me.

What they did do was shift their course, the dark one at the helm. "There's a glass in the bedroom with brandy dregs in it. Was that what Mrs. Barsony gave him to drink?"

"Yes—I guess so. I don't know whether it was brandy or whisky." She was too spent to see the significance of the question. "He'd been drinking before. I could smell it—and Mrs. Barsony said something about finding the bottle out of the cabinet."

"Did they get along all right?"

"Did they——?" She saw it now and could not stem the eagerness within her. Forgive me, Kate Barsony, she begged. "You don't—you're not saying he was poisoned!"

"I'm not saying anything. One guess is as good as another until the autopsy findings are in. You haven't answered my question."

Addie said dully, "What question?"

He rephrased it. "While you and Mrs. Barsony were getting chummy in the park did she let drop how she felt about her son-in-law?"

*My son-in-the-law is a skoonk.* How she had laughed and wept. Much the same impulse seized her now. She coped with it. The voice she produced was false and light. "That would have been a little too chummy on first acquaintance—wouldn't it—considering that I'd never met the man?"

They did not press her further. They turned to face each other as though governed by the same nerve centers. She heard only part of their conversation. It dealt with the fetching of Mrs. Barsony, who had, in the opinion of the sandy-haired one, been gone long enough to put a hundred widowed daughters to sleep. He delegated himself to undertake the mission and left the room.

Addie cleared her throat and addressed the dark one. "Is—is it all right if I go home? I'm a bit tired."

He studied her briefly. She saw herself as he must see her, old and crumpled, an object of pity to anyone with an ounce of pity. She thought that some of the clinical detachment went from his eyes.

He said, "I don't see why not. Sorry we wore you out but that's how it goes. I'll write out my address and phone number for you in case something comes back you might have forgotten to mention."

She could nod to that because she had forgotten nothing. She arose, hoping her stiffened legs would be adequate to the labor of transportation. She reached the hall of the apartment and stood still. The technical crew had emerged from the room where Joe lay and were conferring with the sandy-haired detective. When one of them set down his gear with a thump, Mrs. Barsony stuck her head out of her bedroom door and said in her hoarse carrying voice, "Please do me the kindness not to make such commotions. You disturb my Jancsi."

Addie tried to merge with the wall because she felt that she could endure further conversation with no one. But Kate Barsony saw her and advanced.

"Addie—you go now?" She took Addie's cold hands in hers. "Where do I find the words to thank—or to apologize——?"

"That's all right. How is Jancsi?"

"Still with her eyes wide in spite of sedatives. But I think she begins to thaw. Unlike me she is always an easy weeper—which troubles me that she does not now—though what cause there is for weeping I do not know. I am not enough the hypocrite to call her man a saint simply in that he is dead. Alive he was a villain and now he is a dead villain—and nothing is changed except that his deadness opens for Jancsi the path to a little true happiness. Naturally I have spent sufficient of years in this world to comprehend that love infects most people with a disease of the brains—but I will do my most to nail into Jancsi that who rids her of this miserable husband does her a favor——"

"Shhh," Addie said. But the sandy-haired one had crept up on them, and to her overwrought nerves he seemed to be pointing like a bird dog.

"Why do you shish me, Addie? I regret to offend your fineness but this is the way I feel. Come—I will make some hot nourishment for you. It is the least I can do since you have gone without your dinner on my account." She turned crossly, "Mr. Officer—please not to breathe into my neck."

Addie muttered something and fled. She was not, she thought with a tinge of envy, deserting a sinking ship. Kate Barsony would sail on, no matter what storms arose to batter her.

# 5

Addie did not have her key. She rang the bell and Lindsey opened the door to her. He had put on an old tweed jacket over his tieless shirt. Otherwise his appearance was unchanged. Fearfully she searched his face.

He said, forcing a smile. "It *has* been a long time since we met. Was your Hungarian friend throwing a party for you?"

She followed him to the living room. "It wasn't a party, Lindsey——" She sat down. "It——"

"Well—she had guests anyway—but from the look of you they couldn't have been very stimulating. Elaine went to the door for something and saw a whole mob go in. I hope refreshments were served. We ate long ago."

"Elaine's home?" She asked it almost with indifference. Elaine's threat to leave was lost in a larger threat.

"She's in bed with a headache," Lindsey said.

"I'm sorry she has a headache." Addie moved to the edge of the chair. "Lindsey—that mob she saw was the police. Mrs.

Barsony went for the doctor finally—but by the time he came it was too late——" She was stopped by Lindsey's expression.

"Too late?" he said incredulously. "You don't mean he's gone?" And at her nod, he said, "I don't believe it."

But he did believe it. The incredulity was replaced by something she could not interpret. He walked over to the room's false fireplace. He plucked a pipe from the mantelpiece, placed it between his teeth, and applied a match to the empty bowl. He took the pipe out and looked at it. He spoke, and his speech regained some of its lost Southern coloration, emerging in a drawl. "I've seen many a man look far worse after a fight and live to a ripe old age. Was his heart weak?"

"The police say they can't tell what took him until there's been an autopsy."

"You've been talking to the police?" Lindsey had set the pipe aside. He was lighting a cigarette.

"I was the last person he'd talked to. Naturally they had to ask me if he'd named the—the person who'd given him the beating."

Lindsey said nothing, but she had to look away from him as she added, "He didn't."

Lindsey exhaled smoke and watched it rise to the off-white ceiling. He drawled, "I can't say I'm surprised. The fellow moved in a pretty shady circle. He wouldn't dare name names unless he knew he was bound for the one place he couldn't be reached. And from the glimpse I got of him I wouldn't say that place had figured in his plans." He put out his cigarette and stretched.

She saw him wince. She said quickly, "What is it, Lindsey?"

"A crick in my back. I guess I'm not used to—I guess I don't get enough exercise. Well—I think I'll call it a day. You should, too. You look all in."

"Good night, Lindsey." She made no motion to follow him, and when he reached the door he turned. He said awkwardly,

"Appears I jumped to conclusions about refreshments being served. I could open a can of soup or make a sandwich——"

A day or so ago she would have responded to such thoughtfulness with a gush of gratitude. Now she merely said, "No thank you—I'm not hungry. I'll just sit here for a little bit before I go to bed."

"Suit yourself." Still he stayed. "Was Jan—was his wife there when he died?"

"Not to speak to him. He was unconscious when she came in." With a pang she remembered doubting that stertorous breathing. "And then he—it just happened suddenly."

"I suppose she took it hard."

"Most women would." Her voice was sere.

"Most women would have walked out on Montheil before he had a chance to cause any real grief."

Addie stared at her son, wondering if it were possible that he could make such a statement without thought to the shakiness of his own marital structure. Then it occurred to her that he was not only engaging in conversation with her for the first time since his marriage, but that he was less sparing of words than was his habit. She shuddered at what it had taken to bring this about.

"No sense in sitting there if you're cold," Lindsey said.

She did not hear. She said abruptly, "What's the difference between manslaughter and murder?"

He looked alert but his voice was indolent. "You been learning things from the police? Murder's with malice aforethought. Manslaughter's unintentional I think—like accident resulting in death—or——" His voice changed slightly. "Did the police call it manslaughter?"

"No—they just said it might be."

"Well——" He lounged against the doorjamb, showing, she thought, an odd reluctance to leave her sitting there. "I don't see that it's going to do anybody any good for you to stay up worrying your head about it."

There was so much she wanted to ask him. So much that he might say to ease the insistent ache in her heart. And even if his answers gave no ease they would at least indicate the course that must be followed. It was always better to know what lay in wait. And surely this was her chance, while he stood lingering there. A chance that would seldom if ever come her way again. But she must go carefully. Too often she had seen him retreat into himself at a word or a look that no one else would think to take amiss.

Yet, it was she who retreated at the stern harsh sound of her own voice. "Lindsey—how well did you know Joe Montheil?"

His reply was calm. "Hardly at all. What makes you ask?"

"I—nothing."

"When I was a kid you always told me an answer like that was impolite." To other ears he might have sounded playful. "You always said that folks must finish what they start."

"It was—it was partly your remark about his wife walking out on him—as if you'd got his number."

"Oh that. It wouldn't need much knowing to get his number. I'll bet you got it yourself in the time you spent with him. He probably talked a streak—and most of it lies." The last was tacked on, and held a note of challenge. Self-consciously, he made another postscript. "You always had the gift of seeing clear through to the truth."

She thought that the gift was of small use at the moment.

"Many's the time I can remember being caught out by you." The challenging note was still present. Then he said, "Mother——?"

"Yes?" The syllable was packed with too much hope.

Before its explosive quality he withdrew. Whatever he had been about to say died on his lips. "You won't stay up too long—will you?" This time he implemented his "Good night."

Through the thin walls she could hear his preparations for

bed; the frank outcry of old plumbing, the tinkling of a glass against porcelain, water splashing, the opening of one door, the closing of another, the double thud his shoes made as he dropped them.

For a while after the sounds ceased she sat on, inert except for the churning of her thoughts. It was with difficulty that she summoned the will to drag herself out of her chair, urging her limbs through the motions as though they were rebellious servants over which she had lost control.

Somehow she undressed, and washed her face and hands, and brushed her teeth. And when at last she lay in bed, such a feeling of achievement washed over her that everything else dwindled. She closed her eyes, thinking, Anyone would get the notion I'd put in eight hours of hard labor. At once she fell heavily into sleep.

She did not sleep the night away. It might have been a noise that awakened her, but it could well have been hunger.

For about ten minutes she lay quite still, trying to ignore the demanding hollow that was her stomach. She had never experienced such emptiness. It persisted even though the past day's happenings marched back to fill it with stones. She had placed a glass of water beside her bed. She reached for it and drank. It did no good. And having stirred herself to that extent, she went further. She sat up and lit the light and looked at her watch.

With real despair she saw that it was half-past one. That meant six hours or more of waiting until she could hope for food. The kitchenette, so close by, seemed miles away. Almost passionately she longed for a biscuit, or a piece of dry bread, or a bit of chocolate to lull the pangs. Then her fancy soared to more ambitious heights. She saw a kettle steaming on a little stove. She tasted hot well-buttered toast. It did not end there. Saliva rushed to her mouth as she conjured up food that she told herself no sensible body would dream of eating in the middle of the night, not even if it were available. Fried chicken with cream gravy—spoon bread—steak—— You stop it, Addie. You never were one to cater to yourself. Maybe you're not hungry at all. Maybe it's just nerves. Don't get it into your head that you can start puttering around at this hour. Do you want to disturb everybody?

But it was as though exigence had split her personality, with Mr. Hyde in the ascendant. Why shouldn't they be disturbed? They've disturbed me enough, haven't they? I never asked to be put in the position where I can't blow out my breath without they turn their collars up. They're young. What if I do wake them? The loss of a little rest won't gray their hair. I'm hungry and I'm going to the kitchenette. That's all there is to it.

She deafened her ears to the soft thoughtful argument of the other Addie, stuck her feet into slippers, buttoned her dressing gown, and went. The sky did not fall upon her. She reached goal safely. She put the kettle on for tea. She toasted two slices of stale bread and buttered them lavishly. Because the limited space did not afford a table, she ate standing, with almost sensuous response to each mouthful. But no sooner did her stomach rest content than the aching emptiness broke out in another region.

Carrying her dishes to the sink, she stopped, unconscious that her steps had been arrested by the size and shape of a smoke patch on the wall. That photograph in the Montheil apartment, she thought. No wonder it seemed familiar. It was Joe—Joe Montheil—the way he looked before he—before the accident. As handsome a young fellow as you'd meet in a month of Sundays. She gulped sickeningly, and set the dishes down with a clatter, and held to the sink. The smoke patch became a battered mask, distorted, swollen. She was trying to wash the blood from it and one eye opened——

She gave a little scream as a light hand touched her shoulder. She wheeled in terror to confront Elaine.

Never had she been so glad to see the girl. There she stood, tall and slim and straight, normal as life itself in her pretty robe, with her blond hair loose about her shoulders, and her long greeny-gray eyes sleep-clouded.

"I didn't mean to frighten you," Elaine said.

Addie said tartly, "Next my own shadow will set me jumping." But she was still trembling. "Did I wake you?"

"No. I thought—here—you'd better come inside and sit down for a moment. You're awfully white."

She put her arm around Addie, and Addie leaned, feeling ashamed but not caring much, because human contact was a blessed thing after what had come over her. Elaine switched on the light in the living room and helped her to a chair. Elaine's high brow was shirred into a frown.

"I guess I'm the one to apologize," Addie said. "I went without dinner and——"

"That's all right. I'm sorry I wasn't up to get you something."

She did not seem annoyed, so Addie attributed the frown to other causes. "Lindsey said you had a headache. You run along back to bed or next thing he'll be up to see what's going on."

"No he won't." Elaine hesitated. Then she said in her light clear voice, "He isn't home."

"But it must be nearly two o'clock—of course he's home." In Elaine's eyes she saw the stupid words mirrored. She went on helplessly, "He said good night and I heard him getting ready for bed."

"He came to bed all right. But he didn't stay there. The first time I missed him I was only half awake and I dozed off again thinking he'd gone to the bathroom. By the time I really awoke his side of the bed was cold." There was a kind of gallantry in her shrug, in the loose free stride that took her to the mantel where Lindsey had dropped the packet of cigarettes. She lit one and sat down on the arm of a chair to smoke it. She said, "I shouldn't be doing this—bad for the complexion. I usually have the last one after dinner—unless there's a party or something—not that we've gone to parties lately." And in the same conversational tone, she said, "Funny—this morning I threatened to leave him."

Addie's, "Yes—I know," was involuntary.

The cigarette escaped from Elaine's fingers. She said, "Damn!" and bent to retrieve it, the blond hair swinging forward, hiding her face. "There goes another hole in the rug," she muttered.

Addie wanted to kick herself. "I couldn't help hearing——"

"Just what did you hear?"

"We won't talk about it now. I'll speak to Lindsey as soon as I can find the right moment—and then——"

"There is no right moment to speak to Lindsey," Elaine said. She was standing again. Her face was flushed.

Addie, who had lived in close proximity with her for over a period of months, realized for the first time how young she was, and for the first time glimpsed the trouble that lay beneath her habitual insouciance.

"Sorry," Elaine said. "This is my night to talk too much. I shouldn't even have told you he was out. You've had enough to bear."

As always, Addie's instinct was to give comfort. "What would be the sense of bottling up a thing like that? Besides—I'm sure it doesn't amount to a row of pins. You're not to worry—hear? Likely he couldn't sleep and went out for a walk." *Likely he couldn't sleep,* she thought unhappily. Too likely. She kept her tone sprightly. "I shouldn't wonder you could do with a cup of tea, yourself. Let me get it for——"

"No—sit there." Tears had arisen to the girl's eyes. She gave them no chance to fall. She brushed them away with a clenched hand and said angrily, "Neither of us deserves a bit of kindness from you. We've given you a rotten time."

"Nonsense. I'm sure you had the best of intentions——"

"Don't try to make excuses for us," Elaine said. "There aren't any." She was dry-eyed now, but the flush clung like paint to her fine-textured skin.

"Child—it's not your fault. It's just—just that such arrangements never do seem to work out the way they're planned——"

"Nothing works out the way it's planned." The clear voice held an ancient cynicism. "We're in a mess—the grandfather of messes—and what I don't dare tell him is that I've gone and made it worse——"

Addie's mind was too tired to work. She could not be sure whether the mess referred to was the mess her presence had imposed, or the mess, real or imagined, that dealt with the household next door, or something existing only between Lindsey and Elaine, of which she, Addie, went in ignorance.

"For two pins I'd spill the gory details," Elaine said. "He'd hate me for it but—oh I don't know—I don't know. It had such an innocent start. That card game—a few drinks—a few too many. He falls short for a Southern gentleman. He has no head—he simply has no head—he shows off——"

Addie had closed her tired eyes, the better to concentrate. She knew that she could not afford to miss a word of it. She heard Elaine's footsteps crossing and recrossing the room as she talked, and through her thin eyelids registered the change of light whenever the girl's slim outline passed her chair.

"That's all it was—showing off. Joe dared him—and he did. I could have managed Joe—but he had to drag in that other monster who lost no time in using it for his filthy ends——" Elaine went on and on. Her voice was low and secret. Too low. A soporific. She raised it suddenly. "Is that the door?"

Addie came to with a start. She opened her eyes and focused

them groggily upon Lindsey. He was huddled into his overcoat as though the wind of March had entered with him.

"Welcome home," Elaine said cheerlessly.

Addie experienced no emotion whatever at seeing him safe. Shame left no room for anything else. Elaine had confided in her, and she had heard no more than the first stumbling lines of that confidence. Old fool that she was. Old blundering fool. She had dozed the meat of it away.

# 6

Lindsey said, "What is this—a wake?" and looked with impartial resentment at his mother and his wife. Then he said, "I'm thirsty," and started for the kitchenette.

Behind his back, Elaine murmured, "I think it's a one-man job." She followed him, and because there was nothing else for Addie to do, she took herself back to her room.

She returned to bed, prepared to spend what was left of the night in self-recrimination for having failed Elaine. Miserably, she thought that even if she found the courage to admit that she had dozed the precious confidence away, Elaine would not repeat it. No one, especially one so young and proud, would place trust for a second time in a cracked receptacle. Shame! How could I nod like a senile biddy when it was so important to be alert. A mess, Elaine said. And just the way she said it would have kept anyone awake—anyone but me. If I'm as doddering as this at sixty-odd I've no right to go on living. She gave me my chance to listen and to help and I threw it away. Dear God, make me cunning enough to pretend that I heard, to ask the right questions so that all unaware she'll take me through it again. Lindsey will never tell me. I didn't know how to use my chance with him either. What was it she said before I slept? Something about cards and drinking —something that Lindsey did to show off. And Joe held it over him—no—not Joe—another man. Let me think clearly. I'm not too old to think. There are people in their eighties who hold big important government jobs. I knew from the minute I went next door that something was wrong between Lindsey and Kate—or Kate's family. I knew it because of the way Lindsey behaved when Kate came asking for me. Whatever his faults he always had nice manners toward company.

Her bruised mind strayed. He never could take a dare. When he was seven—or maybe eight—a little girl said he'd be scared to spend the night in that deserted old factory on the outskirts of Gresham. So of course he did spend the night there. And not a word to say for himself when we found him at dawn. What a sorry sight he was—big as a minute and every bit of him scared blue—but do you think he'd let on? Not he —though for once George gave him a good "what's what." George looked a sorry sight, too—hair on end—worried out of his wits. Lindsey was the apple of his eye no matter what they say about fathers being partial to daughters. Not that George didn't love Nanny Lou. Darling Nanny Lou—you never gave us an instant's worry. So smart and sensible—I wish I could talk this over with you. Who could have dared Lindsey from his bed tonight? Where did he go? Not to Joe—Joe's out of the reckoning. He started to call Lindsey a real low-down name and he said he'd put the blame on him but he could have been teasing. Addie Prentice—you old fool—that wasn't teasing. Teasing's a laugh word. Could Lindsey have gone to see the other man—the monster man that Elaine mentioned—Fix? Now how did Fix come into my head? Fix—Jancsi. They stood outside the bedroom door and Fix laughed and she sent him about his business. Fix is no name at all. It only sounded like that. Fix——?

Again sleep surprised her. The room was still dark when next she opened her eyes. She turned on the light and looked in bewilderment at her watch, unable to credit its statement of ten o'clock. Then she became aware of a steady tapping against the windowpane and realized that the darkness was due to rain. Inside the apartment no sound competed with the tapping.

Dressed, she glanced in at the open door of the other bedroom. Obviously, while she slept, the hotel maid had crept in and out. The room was empty and tidy, the spread drawn smooth over the double bed. Its neatness reminded her of the clutter in the Montheil dwelling. She shook her head. She would give thought to nothing until she had eaten breakfast. After that she would call upon Kate and ask if there was anything she could do. After that——?

Elaine had left no note for her. It was ironical, in view of yesterday morning, that she should feel so disappointed. She put coffee on and boiled an egg. She carried her tray to the living room and sat down. She resisted a nervous impulse to bolt the food and get on with whatever the day might hold. She made a slow and civilized meal, telling herself that there was no sense rushing into anything without solid fortification. What she could possibly rush into, she did not pause to ask.

She was washing the dishes when the bell rang. She dried her hands and went to the door, hoping there was enough money in her purse to meet the demands of grocer or cleaner or druggist's boy. She did not recognize the man in the wet trench coat.

"Yes?" she said.

"Good morning, Mrs. Prentice." He took off his hat and bobbed his head politely, but he crossed the threshold without so much as a "by your leave." It was then that his identity became clear. He was the dark member of the detective team. He said, "I don't want to drip on your carpet," and shrugged out of his wet coat. "Could I put this somewhere? It's not such a good morning at that—but I'm not kicking. If it was, you might not be in."

He seemed to consider the call so commonplace, that without a word she took coat and hat and deposited them in the bathroom. He waited for her and paced her to the living room. There, for a moment they stood and looked at each other.

"No use standing when we could be sitting," he said, and forthwith set the example.

She was glad to follow it. She had to clear her throat before she could speak. "I guess you've been across the hall."

"Well—yes—I stopped in there first."

"What brings you here?" She had not meant to speak so bluntly.

"I'm coming to that, Mrs. Prentice. I guess it's going to seem kind of silly but the fact is my partner and I had an argument —and it was about you."

"Me?"

"That's right. Or more exactly a remark of yours. You kind of threw it in and my partner said I couldn't have heard it right."

He's got no call to be here pestering me, she thought, and he knows it. She tried to view him objectively, to ascribe his roundabout approach to lack of ease. She said severely, "The two of you were listening close enough—so I don't see how you could have heard wrong." He looked younger than she had thought him to be last night. He had a cowlick. She was not going to be afraid of anyone with a cowlick. The impression she sought to create was that of a busy woman kept from her work by a nagging schoolboy. "Not that I won't be glad to repeat myself if you'll state your business." She concluded with a cold stare, but it was the coldness of uncertainty. What could she have said. It was what she had not said——

"It was only I thought you mentioned that your son used to be a teacher. I can see by your face that I must have been mistaken."

She hated her face because a detective's reference to Lindsey could affect it. She said, "I guess you *were* mistaken. I didn't say my son used to be a teacher. He *is* a teacher—or rather he's become a supervisor—but it's the same thing because he goes from one school to another and criticizes the work——"

The dark one was nodding soberly. "That's the way my partner made it." He took time out to smooth the cowlick down.

She found the brief silence too long. She threw words into it. "George—my husband—wanted him in the business—but he'd always hankered to be an artist and my husband didn't stand in his way. Only—when he grew up he decided he wasn't good enough—although we both thought he drew and painted real well. So he went in for teaching art instead——"

He interrupted her. "I seem to remember you saying he's employed by private schools."

"No such thing. I didn't get as far as to mention where he taught. I don't believe you were interested at the time—and I can't rightly see why you should be now." Emboldened by her own brusque tones, she went on with a fine recklessness. "But no doubt you have your reasons. After college he went North to study, and the Board of Education gave him a license to teach in high school. If that's all you want to know he's working for the Board of Education to this day."

"No ma'am——"

She waited, because his inflection indicated more to come. Then she said, "No ma'am what?"

It seemed to her that he hesitated. "I mean that isn't all I want to know. In my job there's never an end to knowing. Still

—I guess it's all you can tell me—unless—let's see—while I'm here I might as well make sure I didn't get anything else mixed up. Am I right in thinking yesterday was the first time you met Mrs. Barsony and the Montheils?"

She said, "Seems to me I told you that several times." But there was no vigor in the reproof. She was puzzling over that "no ma'am," which had sounded like a far more significant contradiction than the one he offered in explanation.

"And nobody but you handled the brandy glass beside Mrs. Barsony and the dead Joe?"

She shook her head, wondering how she could have thought his eyes clinical. Now they were nothing but unhappy.

He said, "There were three sets of prints on the glass. We checked the other two—but we found a thumb print that matched the third on a deck of cards in the living room. It also matched one on the arm of the chair where you were sitting."

"Well—I——"

"You didn't play cards yesterday?"

"Of course not."

"But yesterday was your first visit?"

"Cross my heart and hope to——" Then she smiled. "You don't have to give that a thought. I remember now. While I was waiting for you I didn't know what to do with myself so I picked up the room a little. Some cards were scattered on the floor. I put them back in the deck."

He looked her up and down. "I see." His tone did not commit him to belief or disbelief. "I had to ask. If it had slipped your mind that you'd been there before you might have been able to throw some light on Joe Montheil's cronies."

She said truthfully, "I wish I could."

"Well—thanks." He got to his feet.

She brought his coat and hat from the bathroom. As he took them from her she said, "Why do you keep harping on that brandy glass?"

"Harping? I don't know—except in a case like this we harp on everything." His eyes would not meet hers, and yet she had the sensation that he was staring through to her bones.

"Did they discover how—what injury killed Joe Montheil?"

He shrugged. "Who can get the lab to rush things? Could be the higher-ups have been handed some kind of preliminary report—but it hasn't come down to me."

"I should think you'd be informed. You're not an ordinary policeman—are you? At least you're not in uniform."

"I'm a detective-sergeant—which isn't far removed from a uniform. Don't trouble to come to the door."

She went anyway and stood by until he stepped into the elevator. It was not courtesy. She wanted to be sure that he did not go to the Montheil apartment. It would be awkward to run into him there. It would mean that she and Kate could not talk freely. She did not tell herself that her urge to visit Kate was based on other than a purely altruistic motive.

When she was ready, she wore her hat and coat and carried her handbag and her umbrella. If circumstances dictated a short visit she would not return to the apartment. Rain or no rain she would go out. The prospect of being shut in alone all day was to be shunned. She would have faced it on the chance that Elaine might walk in at any moment, but Elaine seldom returned before late afternoon.

She crossed the hall, wishing she knew how Elaine filled those long hours away from home. And this time, because her curiosity held not a drop of censure, she permitted herself to dwell upon it. The answer came with startling suddenness. Of course. It stands to reason! I've been blind about more things than you can shake a stick at. They're short of money. Lindsey must earn more as a supervisor than he did as a teacher —but still—for some reason they're short. To help out Elaine's got herself a job. She felt a glow of affection for the girl, recalling her as she had looked last night. And I had the impudence to think Lindsey had made a poor choice. I only hope the shoe isn't on the other foot. Lindsey? What was that policeman really driving at——?

She curtailed further speculation by knocking resolutely upon the Montheil door. In the few minutes before it was opened she had acknowledged the underlying purpose of her visit. It might be that she could do little for Kate Barsony and Jancsi, but Kate Barsony or Jancsi could do a great deal for her. One of them could give her the name of the other man and so spare her the ordeal of wheedling it from Elaine. Surely that "other man" must have been close enough to Joe Montheil to be familiar to his wife and mother-in-law. The detective should have asked them about Joe's cronies. Not her. But she would pass the name on to him when she had it. She would have to go tactfully. She did not want to harass them at a time like this. But she had to know so that she could rout him out and discover what it was that he held over Lindsey. She had to know, even if it meant harassing the President of the United States. That was all there was to it. Because how else could she be of use? And maybe she would not pass the name on—not if it would hurt Lindsey——

The door opened. Kate Barsony said without enthusiasm, "It is you," and there was no remnant of yesterday's sharing upon her fine-boned face.

"Am I intruding, Kate?"

"The intruding has already been. You wish to enter?"

"Well yes—if——?"

"Be pleased to consider yourself invited."

"Kate—have they—have they taken him away?"

"Oh yes—they have taken."

"When is the funeral? I thought maybe I could——"

"The funeral is when they have taken him apart and presented us with the leavings."

"Jancsi—how is she——?"

"Perhaps within is better for conversing." Kate shut the door behind Addie and ushered her with stiff formality down the hall to the living room. "You will be seated?"

Addie stood, staring openmouthed. The clutter was no longer an expression of carelessness. It had a frenzied air. Desk drawers had been removed and stacked upon a chair. The rug was heaped with their contents. Some of the pictures had been torn from their hooks, exposing squares and oblongs of the wallpaper's original color.

"I beg you to excuse," Kate said. "My hands are too full to attend the housekeeping." She used the tone of a hostess deprecating some minor flaw in her arrangements.

Addie did not try to be tactful. "I thought at first you were moving." A second possible cause for the disorder struck her. "You haven't had burglars too?"

"Perhaps." She spoke as though it were of no consequence. "But if so I find nothing stolen." Her eyes were on the tarnished silver coffee service. "Yet undoubtedly some villain has crept in at the kitchen fire escape during the night when my Jancsi and I lie unconscious with sleep—she by sedatives and I by too much of—of everything. Some mad villain he is—not even an honest thief. That desk I bring from Hungary—it is the one fine piece in this ugly room. The locks upon it can be fixed—but not the scratches he has made in the surroundings."

"That's terrible!" But the scratches were there yesterday, Addie thought fleetingly. Fix didn't go when Jancsi sent him away—he came in here looking for something and he——

"Terrible is comparative. Naturally as soon as I discover—even before I relate the news to Jancsi—I call the police. But they do not become very excited. They send me one of the pair from last night—and also a different specimen who is good enough to come immediately. Yet all that bursts from him is a few important grunts and a few scribblings in his book. Do not however concern yourself. It is but one more little thing. Even the maid from the hotel cannot be bothered with it. She takes a look—throws wide her hands—and turns the tail."

"Kate—what's the matter?" It was wrung from Addie, not by the explanation but by the chill emanating from her friend.

"Matter? I laugh." Distinctly, she said, "Ha—ha."

"Have I done something to offend you——?"

The stern averted face turned toward her. Then it softened. The harsh voice broke. "No, Addie, no. You have not offended. It is the contrary." The softening process descended to her rigid spine. She sagged. "Do you not know that always he who wrongs behaves most injured? On this account only I treat you as if you have come to collect the rent."

Addie's brow was wrinkled with the effort to extract meaning from the words. "You can't have the notion that you've offended me." Her little laugh was poor. "I guess maybe I'm thick-skinned. People have to hit me over the head before I take offense."

"Thick you are not. Do I succeed in casting wool on you when I make like a ramming rod? No. At once you are sniffing a disgusting smell in the place where the wood is kept—and plain as a nose I see there can be no falseness between us. Therefore I will tell you something—though it means you will run from friendship with me when you hear how my Jancsi speaks of your son to the police."

The power went out of Addie's legs. Her umbrella became a crutch. So heavily did she lean upon it that its tip indented the thin worn rug.

# 7

Her voice gained all that her limbs had lost. It seemed to have twice its normal volume. "What does she know of my son?"

Jancsi entered the room, dressed in a soft black robe. Jancsi was like a flower too long exposed to darkness. She said listlessly, "Mother—who—oh——!"

Addie hated her and pitied her. She longed to seize her and shake her. She longed to scream, How dare you bring my boy into this? She said gently, "I hope you're feeling better."

Kate Barsony's back had straightened. Her hoarse voice boomed. Addie was not its target. She addressed the air above her daughter's drooping head. "Is there need to inquire how she feels? Look at her—white as the flour for the Easter bread. I ask of heaven what shall I do with this girl? Has she eaten the fine breakfast I prepare? No—it sits untouched on the bedside. And will she rest calm on her behind to recover the good gift of health and brain which I give her at birth? No——"

"Mother——"

"No—I say. She must wander into where she is not wanted —especially last night when the policemen do not insist to degree her but are content to wait until such a moment as she can recover her senses and will not splash on them like a hose histories which cause harm to the neighbors and joy to nobody. And for what? For a man who when he dies must await the permission of the police to be buried—nor do they even inform me at what day to anticipate his funeral. But one thing is certain. Should his wife continue in this way she will be unable to attend—and that is a disgrace——"

It was Addie who cried, "Don't!" The girl was drifting from the room, a more convincing Ophelia than the actress who had played the role when Nanny Lou got the tickets for nothing and said they might as well go. Suppose that Nanny Lou's Tom had been—had been——? "Nanny Lou," Addie said, "Jancsi——" She went to the girl and took her unresisting hand. "Your mother doesn't mean to be unkind. She just wants to help you. You hurt real bad now but time will——" She stopped, seeing the stock words for what they were, as hard and comfortless as rented chairs. She tightened her grip on the cold hand, seeking thus to impart her message of sympathy.

"Thank you." Jancsi's low voice was a pulse, throbbing and uneven. "I didn't mean to do you harm—but Joe—no matter what he was or what he did—that—that was no way for him to die. You were kind to him—my mother told me how you——" She choked. From under her lowered eyes, half screened by the heavy lashes, tears began to flow. Men wept that way sometimes, fighting every step of the way, the sobs increasing in violence at each attempt to restrain them.

Kate Barsony suffered yet another sea change. She swooped. She pinioned the girl to her and all but flew with her to the couch. She cradled her and rocked her back and forth. She crooned a weird lullaby. "There now—weep—it is well—it drains the poison from you—my darling—my baby—my bird—it is for this your mother's words are sharp—to perform like the surgeon—to cut and let out the black festering—there now—there——"

Unable to breathe in that dense emotional air, Addie escaped. She found the kitchen. When she returned with a glass of water the sobs had dwindled. Jancsi was able to say, "Thank you," to sip dutifully, to twist from her mother's embrace, to dry her eyes on the flowing sleeves of her robe.

"See," Kate Barsony said, "this is more like herself. Always from a little child she forgets the handkerchief." The simple words were a mixture of pride and relief and rebuke, just such an utterance as must have dealt with her brood when they were new, and life less complicated.

Jancsi smiled shakily. Her beautiful, slightly uptilted eyes were washed clean of the film they had worn since the death of Joe Montheil. "I think—I think I'd like a cup of coffee—and then I'll dress and get some air——"

"Coffee you shall have, my brave one—and food with it—but out you do not go in this rain. Enough is plenty." Kate strode to the kitchen.

Addie saw Jancsi's mouth firm, saw the softly rounded chin take on a more definite curve. It made her think that the last word had not been said upon the subject of going out. Then her own problem, but lightly buried by the little scene, was exhumed. Bleakly she contemplated it. Could she question the girl after what she had been through? Her outward eye settled blankly upon the stacked desk drawers.

Jancsi was watching her. Jancsi said, "I suppose you're puzzled about—about a great many things."

Addie was puzzled about one thing only. The curve of Jancsi's chin encouraged her to express that which related to it. "I want to know what you said to the police. A detective came to see me this morning. He didn't mention you—he went through some rigmarole—but he must have come because of what you told him."

"I'm sorry—I'm truly sorry—I was confused last night—and Lindsey was the only one I could think of who'd have reason to—well—he *was* mixed up in it—and I couldn't leave him out just because he happens to be your son."

It was reasonable, but not to Addie. "How was he mixed up in it?"

"Don't you—hasn't he said?"

"No."

"Then I'd rather not."

"You must." Addie tempered it. "I won't blame you. I guess it's natural you should be loyal to your husband and want to do all you can to clear up the—the way he met his death. I can understand that."

"No you can't—not if you start off by thinking it's natural. It isn't. Mother doesn't understand either. Mother——"

The words were a thick wood to Addie. She tried to chop her way through. "All I'm asking you is——"

Jancsi went on as though she had not spoken. "You see—Mother thinks I loved Joe——"

"Look—will you please tell me——" But Addie was trapped. "Your mother thinks——? Didn't you love him?"

"I loved him at first—and again for a few moments last night when—when he was lying there—but there was a big empty space between." The sigh she gave was thin and wispy as though it had nothing to feed upon. She said, "Even last night's love didn't last."

Addie's voice was bitter. "Then you're right—I don't understand—I really don't understand why you——"

Jancsi arched her exquisite small body. She might have been straining against constricting fetters. "Guilt. You can laugh if you like. I used to laugh at the labels too. I was the only one of my friends who didn't fall for Freud. I used to laugh a lot at everything. I don't now. There's nothing to laugh at—and hasn't been—and won't be." She lifted her head high. "But there'll be nothing to cry at—and that's—that's some compensation."

Addie went on chopping. "I don't see why you should feel guilty unless you lied to the police about——"

"It isn't that. I'm guilty because I failed and it's all been such a waste. Way down inside of me I always knew what Joe was like—but I thought I could change him—and I couldn't. I failed because I must have done the wrong things. Oh I know they say you can't change people and it's a mistake to try—but that can't be true if you love enough—and I didn't—and I was stupid—and that's why I've got to do something for him now—to make up for not being able to help him when he was here. He'd hate—it wouldn't be fair to let him dwindle into just another of those unsolved cases. His ego couldn't—couldn't rest if I sat still and didn't lift a finger. And it isn't as though he was really bad. He was lazy and weak and so long as my money lasted he'd never have tried to get a job—but I think his sins were all on a petty scale until he met Lindsey and Elaine."

Addie made silent reappraisal of Elaine in the light of that after-midnight performance, and pronounced her innocent. If she's going to accuse Elaine too then none of it's true. But she said nothing, fearing to send Jancsi off again on an excursion through her inner dark.

"We'd seen them around," Jancsi said, "and when Joe asked them in for bridge and they came I was very pleased. They seemed more like the people I was used to than—well—Joe had a habit of picking up anybody and he'd been spending far too much time with—with one particular person. I thought that having nice friends in the same hotel might break that up——"

One particular person, Addie thought, yet dared not interrupt to ask his name.

"I don't drink a lot, myself," Jancsi said. "Elaine and I had one highball—and Joe and Lindsey drank the rest of a bottle of scotch. Pretty soon they got too tight to know what they were doing so we had to stop playing bridge. Then——"

Kate, stay in the kitchen, Addie prayed. Please don't come out yet.

"Then Joe began to tell dirty stories—and Mother—she'd been sitting on the couch sewing—went to her room. Not that she's a prude—but I guess you have to like people to stand them when they're vulgar—and she had no reason to like Joe. He'd led her a pretty miserable life—so his vulgarity just embarrassed her. Not that he cared if she went or stayed. He was out to shock Lindsey because schoolteachers are supposed to be so proper—but Lindsey wouldn't shock. Instead, after a few more drinks he started to top Joe in kind of a bored way—just to prove he wasn't a stuffed shirt I guess. The two of them forgot that Elaine and I were there. We didn't like it. We tried to change the subject but we couldn't. When they ran out of stories Joe started to draw pictures on the score pad, and Lindsey made some remark about them, and Joe said, 'Let's see if you can do better—go on—I dare you.' And Lindsey took over the pad and pencil.

"Elaine and I went over to the couch. We talked about different things but I know we were each thinking of some way to call it a night. It would have to be something subtle—people get so stubborn when they're drunk. I made coffee but they refused it. Joe was laughing his head off. Every once in a while he'd yell something like, 'You're a genius—a regular Rembrandt—if I had your talent you wouldn't catch me teaching brats,' and he kept asking for Lindsey's autograph. Lindsey would write it with a flourish and Joe would take the drawings he'd signed and put them in his wallet—carefully—as though they were masterpieces." She wrinkled her nose. "Elaine was pretty uncomfortable—although she doesn't show much—does she? She hadn't seen the drawings but she could imagine what they were like. So could I. I meant to sneak them away as soon as I had a chance—and tear them up—not for any reason except that I didn't want things like that around. It didn't occur to me that there could be a stronger reason for getting rid of them until afterward——"

Kate came in with a heavy tray. She said, "I have prepared a little lunch." She set the tray down near Jancsi, happened to glance at Addie's face, and went on talking. "But getting my hand back into the cookery gives me a tremendous appetite so I am impatient and have stuffed myself up in the kitchen. Now I go to freshen the bed for my little one since the best occupation she can engage in on such a dirty day is sleep." Jauntily she left the room again.

Noting the service for three upon the tray, Addie blessed her. In part payment, she poured coffee, heaped Jancsi's plate with omelet, and took a token portion for herself. Jancsi ate as one who performs a tiresome but essential chore. She continued to speak as though there had been no break in her recital.

"Finally," Jancsi said, "Elaine got Lindsey to leave—but I had no luck in handling Joe. He said the night was young and why shouldn't we go places and enjoy it. By that time I was sick of being subtle. I nagged him to get undressed and into bed—which was exactly what I shouldn't have done. He called me a crepe-hanger and he said I could do as I pleased but life was too short to sleep away——" It was not omelet that she swallowed. "So it ended by his dashing out alone. It was quite late—after one—and he was in no condition to be wandering the streets—but I was more angry than worried. You see—I had a fair idea where he'd head—about the only place he'd find anyone at that hour. I'd forgotten the drawings entirely—but of course he had them with him—and of course he must have dragged them out and shown them to—to the first person he met."

Jancsi stirred the remaining coffee in her cup but did not drink it. "There was no more bridge-playing with Elaine and Lindsey." From the tone of her voice this might have been the major outcome of the whole affair. "I wouldn't be surprised if Elaine thought I was—was a party to it from the beginning. She'd hardly smile at me when we ran into each other in the lobby or the elevator. Then one day I came home and found Lindsey here—and it wasn't a social call. He and Joe were quarreling like mad. I heard just the end of it but I heard enough to know it had to do with those ugly stupid drawings." Again she gave that wispy little sigh. "It wasn't much fun being married to a blackmailer," she said.

The full stop was implicit in the somber fall of her voice and in the way she set her cup and plate upon the tray.

Addie needed a brake for her spinning thoughts. She seized the word, "Blackmail." "Who would blackmail Lindsey? He has no money except what he earns as a teacher—and everyone knows how far that goes."

"I can't help it if it sounds crazy. Maybe he—maybe Joe thought he could get money somewhere. If Joe hadn't thought something he—he'd be alive."

"Surely," said Addie, "surely you're not accusing Lindsey of being responsible for Joe's death." She drew breath experimentally, as though once the question was out relief would follow. She was like a patient who has submitted to the removal of a tumor. But there was no relief, and would not be until examination proved the tumor benign.

Jancsi was brushing invisible crumbs from her robe. Jancsi said, "I only know his death was connected with some sort of crookedness——"

"This story you've told me—is it what you told the police?"

"I guess so—in substance anyway. Mother was trying to stop me and she fussed—and the police doctor had given me a shot of something—and the policemen were shouting at her—and that dark one was staring at me as if he'd never seen a woman before—and finally I couldn't say anything at all. I wish—I wish now I hadn't tried to say anything in the first place—to you or the police. I wish Lindsey weren't your son. I wish things didn't get so complicated that everything everybody did or said involved everybody else."

You guess so—and you wish, Addie thought bitterly. You egg the police on to my son and all you can do is guess or wish. "What's the name of the other man?" The words struggled out of her tight throat.

"Other man?"

Addie hammered away at the inimical quality that had crept into Jancsi's eyes. "The one Joe was seeing too much of—the one he showed the drawings to. You didn't hesitate to bring Lindsey into it—so you wouldn't have left the other man out when you talked to the police—not if you've been truthful in what you said about failing Joe when he was alive and wanting to make up for it now."

Jancsi was looking at her delicate hands. Jancsi's beautiful mouth was pursed. She opened it to say in an incredibly casual voice, "Oh yes—I know the man you mean—but he has nothing to do with this matter—because there's no possible reason why he and Joe would fight. They were bosom friends." She appeared to think that she had fulfilled whatever obligation she might have toward Addie. She started to rise. "If you'll excuse me I'll——"

"You haven't finished," Addie said. "I won't excuse you until you give me his name——"

Jancsi was walking toward the hall, purposefully, all traces of Ophelia shed. Desperately, Addie tried to hold her, rushing to stand between her and the door. "Was he the one I heard you talking to outside the bedroom—the one you called 'Fix'?"

"Fix?" It was the same inflection she had used in repeating, "Other man."

"Yes—Fix. You know exactly who I'm talking about. It was Fix you called him—or near enough——"

"Please——" There was nothing inimical in Jancsi's eyes. There was only appeal. "Please believe me—it wouldn't do any good for you to know. Let me——"

"Let you what? Do more damage to Lindsey so that you can protect——?"

But Jancsi had darted past her. Jancsi was gone. Jancsi was tripping down the hall, and a moment later a door had closed and a lock had clicked and there was the sound of a flowing tap.

All right, Addie thought grimly. All right, my girl. I'll wait. You can't stay there forever.

She sat down, her eyes wandering once more to the region of the desk, to the deep scratches around the forced locks. Everything pointed to Fix, she thought. The scratches had not, as Kate supposed, been made by the after-midnight invader. Kate had simply been too preoccupied to see them yesterday. But she, Addie, had seen them. Kate was out when Jancsi entered the bedroom. So what had there been to prevent Fix from prowling about if there was something he wanted to find. Something? Of course—Lindsey's drawings. And where else would he seek them but in a locked desk? Maybe he'd panicked and fled after the beating and returned with a cooler head. She was so sure of Fix as the criminal now that she might have been witness to his brutal attack upon Joe. Bosom pal indeed! A man with a laugh like that was nobody's bosom pal. But he must have been interrupted when Kate came in with the doctor. He must have hid and let himself out quietly when they were all in the bedroom. And he must have returned last night to get what he was after. How's that for a clear piece of reasoning, old lady? But because of the one large flaw in it she was unable to accept her own congratulations.

Grown men—especially grown men like Fix and Joe—did not blackmail people for spite. And why else would they do it—with Lindsey poor as a church mouse? His job being what it was, they could hold the drawings over him, have him dismissed, disgraced. But wasn't that a lot of trouble to go to unless they were out of their heads? Joe hadn't been out of his head. He had been—what was it they called them in the movies—a smart operator. No question about it. And probably Fix was even smarter. And that was bad—since he now possessed the drawings and intended to use them for heaven only knew what purpose. She refused to condemn Lindsey for the drawings, having thrust aside her immediate reaction to them as nothing but the prudish conditioned response of a small-town mind. They were childish, that was all. Any halfway sensible person would realize that. The sort of thing kids do almost as soon as they can manage a pencil. Usually they scribbled words. But Lindsey was never much for words. Because of too many drinks, and because Joe had encouraged him, he had behaved like a foolish child. The best of men were childish once in a while, and maybe the drawings weren't so bad as Jancsi made them out to be. Young girls were often apt to go nice-nellyish if it suited them. Young girls? Jancsi was a married woman. Jancsi was a widow. And Lindsey——? Oh Lindsey! A new horror visited her.

Her head began to pound. Yesterday, when Lindsey got so angry with Joe and dashed out, there had been as much chance for him as for Fix to come into the living room and try to force that desk. And where had he gone last night if not to finish——? She pressed her hands to her head. I won't give it another thought. It was Fix. I'll just have to make Jancsi give me his real name so that I can see him. Has she come out of the bathroom? I forgot to listen. Is that——?

But it was Kate she heard walking up the hall. Kate entered the room wearing coat and hat and little boots for the rain. "Jancsi now bathes," she said, with the air of conveying an important bulletin. "When she is ready she will agree to go back to bed instead of to walk in the wetness. But she wishes some magazines to read for her distraction—and also cigarettes, which she should do without—yet I am a piece of putty with no heart to refuse her." She glanced at the tray. "Good—you have made her swallow something. The dishes will stay until I return—and also I leave this whole disgraceful mish-mosh for later." Then she said, "You have talked together with her? You have perhaps found that after all she does not spill too many beans to the police?"

Addie said with dignity, "There weren't any beans to spill."

"I cannot tell you how this relieves me. I take a lesson—and next time do not boil like a teapot for no reason."

No reason, Addie thought, unable to credit that airy dismissal of death and murder and suspicion.

"Since you have your umbrella perhaps you will join me in the shopping. Perhaps we stop in at the grocery also."

"Wouldn't you rather I gave you a hand at straightening up?"

"Oh no. Once I begin to tackle it takes no time at all. Meanwhile it will not eat bread."

Kate was eying her expectantly, and a little air, even wet air, might ease her aching head. And she had a feeling that so long as she sat there waiting, Jancsi would cling to her refuge of the bath. But Jancsi might not expect her to return, and——

Kate misinterpreted her hesitancy. "Do not consider me rude to push you from the house. It is understood we come back here and spend the afternoon. Yes?"

"Yes," said Addie. She arose. "That will be—that will be a pleasure."

# 8

Kate Barsony halted at the desk to see if there was any mail. Addie expected nothing because correspondence with the Gresham folks had tapered off, and Nanny Lou's bimonthly letter had arrived a few days ago. She walked on toward the exit wishing that the hotel boasted a newsstand in the lobby. Then she could read about yesterday, and Kate could buy cigarettes and magazines, without having to quit the building. It seemed important to get back upstairs before Jancsi discovered some new way to evade her.

She leaned against a pseudo-marble column and waited. Kate seemed to be spending a long time at the desk. She turned and saw her talking to the manager. Or rather, the manager was talking to her. Kate had assumed the attitude of royalty being forced to cope with a peasant. It was the manager's policy to dodge demands and complaints by lying low, but Addie could guess the reason for his being on view now. He was probably taking Kate to task for her son-in-law's abuse of the Vauban's hospitality. Distressed, hoping that Kate would maintain her royal aloofness, Addie was about to go to her aid when she saw Jancsi.

Her first impulse was to alert Kate. Her second, which she obeyed without examination, sent her behind the column. But Jancsi, who had just stepped out of the elevator, glanced neither to the right nor the left. Her passage to the door and into the street was straight and swift.

Addie emerged and started to pursue. She jumped as Kate grasped her arm. There had been no need to play the informer. Kate's hoarse voice muttered in her ear, "Hurry—we do not let this serpent's tooth escape."

They reached the street in time to see Jancsi walking east. She had covered half the block.

The two ladies slogged through the sharp rain, managing to keep their will-o'-the-wisp in sight. Kate did not save all her breath for the exercise. She panted, "Without even goulashes she walks—without even the raincoat and the umbrella. And she has presented me with such a pure face when she agrees to stay at home. I wash my hands—it is too much. Addie—keep your eyes open for a cab—we will take the driver into a portion of our confidence and say she is sick and ask him to crawl slowly behind that harm will be prevented from coming to her. She will take sufficient harm from the way I fix her when——"

Addie managed to open her mouth. "Kate—who is Fix——?"

"Who is——? Addie—you are well? Do we hurry too fast for you? Wait—here is a cab—quick—no—it has customers. We must be awake for one with its top light burning which means empty."

But all the cabs were full, so they struggled on. In one way the rain favored them. There were no crowds abroad to hide Jancsi from their wet straining eyes.

Addie's umbrella wavered in her cold hand. It dislodged Kate's hat, but Kate only said temperately, "Give it here—I am the taller." She held the umbrella too high to do either of them any good, and resumed her running commentary. "Does this changeling seek to lead us on a tour of the universe? First she turns down the Americas' Avenue for how many blocks I cannot count—and now once more she makes across the town. If she takes a bus on Fifth Avenue it roasts our goose—no? Ah——?"

Jancsi did not reach Fifth Avenue. She entered a tall building three doors from the corner.

Kate said triumphantly, "The chasing narrows. We shall soon see what she is up to."

But inside the building optimism faded. The vast tiled lobby was divided into three corridors, each with its bank of elevators. And there was nothing to indicate which corridor Jancsi had used, or which elevator was bearing her upward.

"Perhaps the direction board tells us something," Kate said, pointing with the umbrella. They planted themselves before the large glassed-in square and studied it until the white letters danced on the black background. Acme this—Acme that—Antiques, Ltd.—Basket Guild—Beauty Incorporated—Bell—Century Clothes—Colorfast Fabrics—Durwood Electrical Appliances—Eastern Sales—Foam—Freedman Togs—Highwide Games—L. S. Kincaid—King—Lightbourne Sports Apparel—Newbury—J. C. Newman, C.P.A.—Pandora Jewelry—Photomatics—Pine's Paper Co.—Quinn's Bras—Randleman & Son—Rankin—Rolf—Rush—Spheres Publishing Co.—Stamps of the World—Sugarsweet—Sunbeam Studios—Surgical Braces—Trimble—Wall——

They gave it up, turning disconsolately to each other. Kate muttered, "Formidable—a census-taking of the city——"

Addie said without hope, "Don't you see anything suggesting where she might——?"

Kate shook her head vigorously. "No—but she must come down. This is ultimate. So we wait. We choose a strategical vantage place and we wait. At least we are in out of the rain." She observed her companion's sodden appearance and accepted it as a reflection of her own. "I mean what rain we have not brought in with us."

They wandered toward the line of revolving doors that gave onto the street. Kate left Addie for a few minutes and came back bearing a carton of cigarettes, several magazines, and a newspaper. She said sheepishly, "So long as I have set out to buy them I do it."

"Kate—may I see the newspaper?"

"Of course. I myself have already glanced. Fortunately it makes no headlines. On the third page—I think."

The short account of Joe Montheil's death took no time at all to read. Lindsey was not mentioned in it. Addie, herself, was referred to as a neighbor. She gave the paper back to Kate.

"At the stall where I bought this," Kate said, "I have also conversed with the young man who sells. Most young men observe Jancsi even should she wear green in a thick forest—but I am afraid this one misses some of his genes since he fails to recognize her by my description. However he supplies the information that this building runs through to the next street so perhaps we wait in vain since Jancsi is quite inconsiderate enough to escape us that way. I tell you never from the time they are tiny scraps of creatures have I laid a rough hand upon my children—but at this moment—no matter what her years—I am tempted to give Jancsi everything she has earned were I another type of parent. Addie—Addie—what is it? What happens to your face?"

"Nothing—I——" She tried to say it naturally—to look natural once it was said. "I reckon I'm just wet and miserable—and I have a slight headache."

"You should have mentioned—I would not drag you out. I go back at once to the young man and purchase aspirin and find a water fountain. It will dismiss the headache and fortify against catching a cold. I intend to swallow a tablet myself to keep you company."

Addie did not hear her. Addie's eyes were glued to the last revolving door, the one through which her son had just made his exit. She had seen him all right. It had been no mistake, no trick of vision. She knew her son even with his back bent under an invisible weight, and his young face so tortured that it made her want to weep.

It is Thursday, she thought. A school day. And what is he doing away from his work? What is he doing in this building? Coincidence? Or had he arranged to meet Jancsi? But what could Jancsi and he have to say to each other? They were enemies. She had given his name to the police. The police—the dark detective. The "No ma'am" that had been so puzzling. What was it he said? Something like, "Seems to me your son teaches in one of those private schools." And she, "He's with the Board of Education." And then, "No ma'am——" Did that mean he had checked and discovered that Lindsey no longer was employed by the Board of Education? Had he been—had he resigned because he feared that those pictures, drawn in drunkenness, would come to light and disqualify him as a suitable mentor for youth? Go after him! Ask him! But she could not. She could not let her proud contained son know that she had caught him off guard, seen him abject, defeated, stooping beneath some unsupportable burden.

"I wouldn't be surprised if Elaine thinks I was party to it from the beginning," Jancsi said. And maybe Elaine did think so, and maybe it was true. And maybe Jancsi's fierce little air of integrity was a lie. Outward beauty gave people a head start. Everyone was much too ready to believe the best of it, in spite of the fact that again and again it had proved misleading. But——? If Lindsey and Jancsi had agreed to meet here, why hadn't they come together? Neither of them knew there was anyone around to spy upon them.

Addie went back to the directory. Somewhere behind those innocent-seeming names, Fix was hiding. Fix, the hated symbol of all despair. Fix Bell—Fix Durwood—Fix Kincaid—Lightbourne—Newbury—Newman—Rankin—Spheres . . . Come out, you sneak—you monster——! Again the white letters met and parted in a crazy dance. Fix Acme—Acme—Acme. . . . When she turned away she felt that on demand she could have recited every name on the board.

A worried Kate stood near the exit. "I start to think I lose you also," she said as Addie joined her. Gratefully, Addie accepted the aspirin, the dripping paper cup, and wished that she were free to complete the treatment with endless sleep in a deep bed, and every blind drawn tight.

"We go home to dry clothing now," Kate said decisively, "and there await what big story Jancsi brings to us."

They were both surprised to find that the rain had stopped. Kate tilted her head back to search the sky. "You think it clears for good?" she said.

"I don't know." Nor did she care. But the crisp washed air was kind to her pounding temples. Suddenly, damp as she was, she felt reluctant to go home. She had no hope that Lindsey would be there, not if he was determined to keep his absence from school a secret. As for Jancsi? If Jancsi had allied herself with Fix it was madness to expect help from her. No matter. There was still Elaine. With the information now in hand, Elaine need never know that her confidence had been poured into sleep-deafened ears. Yes, she must be patient until she saw Elaine, who could supply the name that cored everything. Meanwhile—meanwhile——? She turned to Kate. Kate might not know Fix by name but surely, provided the right questions were asked, she would be able to supply some clue to his identity.

"Kate," she said urgently.

Kate halted. "You, too?"

"I—"

"Never mind—I am in full accord. I merely refrained from mention because with your head I believed you wished to hasten home. But it is stupid to remain distressed when there is a very nice 'Ladies' in that hotel on the other side. I know for I have patronized it before." Disregarding the traffic light, she took Addie's arm and piloted her safely across the street.

It *was* a very nice "Ladies." It was, in fact, a very nice hotel, and the considerate management had provided good chairs and dressing tables and mirrors for the convenience of guests. Comforted, Addie and Kate produced their compacts and combs and labored to improve their bedraggled state.

"You begin to grow pinker," Kate said approvingly. "Perhaps not aspirin but only a helping hand to nature has relieved your head. If my ship arrives I move here to repay for the hospitality. Meanwhile we will make a deposit by eating a little bite in the tea and coffee emporium in the basement. It is inexpensive. On occasion I have tried it when I desire to waste time—but how much happier it will be with you for conversation."

Addie thought that the "Ladies" was as good a place as any for the conversation she had in mind. Better than a crowded tea room. She said, "I'm not a bit hungry."

"Do not tell me this. By the tray I prepared I noticed that Jancsi stuffed like a pig but that you touched nothing—unless it was vice versa."

"No—Jancsi ate—but I'd had a hearty breakfast."

"Breakfast is long ago. Now it is past the luncheon hour." She consulted the enameled watch pinned to her lapel. "Would you believe—already it is half after two o'clock. Come."

Addie could make no further protest because she owed Kate a treat, and had owed it since a year ago yesterday in the Vienna Shop.

The restaurant below stairs offered almost as much privacy

as the "Ladies." The few remaining lunchers were at the dessert stage, and the waitress who took Kate's order was grudging at first. But Kate's expansive friendliness made her smile and forget to act as though she were being put-upon. Kate prescribed hot chicken soup to be followed by a fresh fruit salad, and Addie discovered that she could still eat.

Kate spooned the last of her soup and started on the salad. She speared a slice of pineapple and regarded it with satisfaction. "Having lately been close to death—you and I," she said, "there are those who might consider us without heart to sit here and enjoy—especially me. Yet—what is done is done—and as I say to the police detectors—dying does not improve a man's character—and underneath the circumstances grieving is pretending."

"You shouldn't have said that to the police, Kate——"

"But why—it is the truth."

"I know—only they might——"

"Figs for what they might!" Then she said quietly, "It is sufficient for me to know that although sometimes my temper breaks away—never do I have murder in my heart."

Addie gave it up. Even for those whose business was suspicion, Kate as a murderer must be a concept too ludicrous to entertain. She set her fork upon the plate as precisely as though some authority on etiquette were whispering instructions in her ear. She said, "What exactly did Jancsi tell the police about my son?"

Kate sighed. "I regret I am tactless enough to remind you of this subject. You wish to discuss it? Very well—we discuss—but please do not permit it to sour your food. What Jancsi exactly said I cannot report. I am too busy with interrupting her to listen. I can however assure you that I do not let her progress very far. She states your son's name—Lindsey Prentice—and says he has quarreled with Joe Montheil on the dirtiness of picture-drawings for which the scoring paper from bridge is used. I think that even if the detectors can make some heads and tails with this they will soon find other more important ways to occupy themselves—for I have informed them that I can name at least a dozen who quarrel with Joe Montheil."

Addie leaned across the table. She said intensely, "Can you?"

Kate looked distressed. "Well—no—but it is logic to suppose they exist from how this late skunk comports himself."

That was no longer even remotely funny. It induced neither laughter nor tears.

"Addie—you sit there so solemn I begin to be ashamed all over again—just as I am when you knock upon the door this morning. It is evident you cannot actually forgive me for Jancsi's mischief to your son."

"There's nothing to forgive. You did the best you could to stop it—but right now——"

"Still more would I do if called upon. But I comfort me they are not interested in dirty pictures. They are interested in murders—and I propose this is merely an accident Joe Montheil causes to happen by crossing his eyes at someone he does not expect to be so prepotent."

"It *is* murder, Kate——"

"Let it be murder then—so long as Jancsi is now a widow and so long as your son is safe. Addie—please do me the kindness not to remain so sad in the face."

"Won't you try to understand? My son isn't safe—he——"

"Poof! To look at you is to know that you could not make a baby who grows up to murder." Then her bright eyes widened and she said in a shocked voice, "Addie—can it be you have some secret fact which leaves me in the darkness?"

"It is the other way around. You——"

"I?" She looked very troubled. "You think I do not lay my cards upon your table?"

"Yes—no wait—you're not keeping anything back on purpose—but Kate—you see only one side of this—this terrible thing. For you it means only that Joe was not a suitable husband for Jancsi and that now he's out of the way——"

"What else is to see?"

"My side of it—Lindsey's side of it."

"Believe me—this also I keep track of."

"But the detective questioned me this morning. He wouldn't make a special trip to do that unless it was very serious for Lindsey."

"Is this why you disturb yourself? It is not serious—I promise. Everyone is questioned. For example, the manager ——" Kate held her nose, released it, and went on, "Also the other tenants upon our floor—also the elevator driver—the sweepers—everyone. And should the Vauban contain infants in their carriages I am not surprised if they are asked for their two-centses." She stared at Addie hopefully, shrugged, and sighed. "Very well—I become solemn with you. What is it you believe I conceal? Mention and I produce."

"When I was talking with Jancsi she referred several times to some man Joe had been hobnobbing with—some man she didn't cotton to——"

Kate interrupted apologetically, "What is this hobnobbing and cotton?"

Addie began again. "Joe had been seeing a lot of some man. When I asked his name Jancsi changed the subject. Kate—you've got to help me—you must have met him—he must have come to visit with Joe at least once when you were home. Please, Kate—think."

"I do not require to think. I place this specimen immediately. He visits not once but often when I have the misfortune to be at home. Yet if you have in your mind that he kills Joe Montheil in such a way—then I must disappoint you, Addie. For he is flabby like noodles dripping with butter."

"What's his name?"

"Do not bite off my head or I find it impossible to say. His name is Mr. Felix Watling."

Addie leaned back in her chair. She repeated weakly, "Mr. Felix Watling." Then she said, "No."

"You are familiar with him?" Kate said.

"He called on Lindsey and Elaine a short while after I arrived in New York. He and his wife." Lindsey had introduced the pair as Mr. and Mrs. Watling. Her memory struggled to reconstruct them. The woman, a girl really, had wielded a heavy hand in the cosmetics' department. She was what Gresham folk would have described as "fast." And the chief impression left by the man had been polish, of manner, of fingernails, and of shoes. Felix? Fix? She tried to associate Mr. Watling with the crude masculine laugh she had heard outside Joe's room. She shook her head, recalling his speaking voice, deliberate and smooth. And having recalled his voice, other details came to her, his indoor complexion, his lack of stature, his well-tailored clothes designed to minimize a tendency toward corpulence. He had greeted her very civilly. He had even cracked a pompous little joke when he caught her glancing at her watch. She had been wondering how soon she could retire because she blamed her presence for the absence of ease in the room, and to cover her embarrassment she had told him that the watch was her most prized possession because her husband had given it to her on their last wedding anniversary. Right after that he had withdrawn his attention, almost, she thought, as though a tiresome but necessary social obligation had been successfully discharged. Beyond an initial and nasal, "Pleased to meet you," his wife had said nothing at all to anyone. Later, Addie had told herself that she could not expect New Yorkers to be the same as the folks in Gresham. They were more sophisticated, and there was no reason to feel hurt because they did not make talk with a country cousin. Besides, Mr. Watling was a big important man.

Lindsey had as good as said so in his introduction. He had said that Mr. Watling was a—was a——?

"Addie—Addie—for the second time I am repeating that if this individual has a wife she makes news to me. I am surprised if he has a mother."

Addie said, "But I met his wife."

"Hmmm—a little penny cake he picks up on some corner. Men like him must always soothe their vanity with the lie that they are irresistible—and since any woman of self-esteem laughs on them they content themselves with the other type. Marry them they do not—in case the real thing falls into their lap one day. I give you a sample when I tell you that beneath Joe Montheil's nose I have seen this Watling make the greedy eye at Jancsi."

Addie said stubbornly, "She was introduced to me as Mrs. Watling——"

"She was respectable?"

"Well——"

"Naturally. Therefore your son introduces her as Mrs. because he is ashamed and needs an excuse to present his mother with such a penny cake."

"But——" Addie was teased by a thin ray of hope. No one had addressed Mr. Watling by his first name—not even his wife. She clung to the wife's bona fides because to do so was essential to her premise. Watling was not a common name, but even so he might not be Felix or Fix at all. He might be innocent kin to the burly monster with the ugly laugh. She set her lips. The one who had beaten Joe to death. "What does your Felix Watling look like?" she demanded.

"My Felix Watling? Do not give him to me, please. I give him right back. He is like in the song—a Mr. Five by Five clad in expensive haberdashery which in his case is money thrown away. He is a shabby piece of furniture all shined up that it may fool someone into buying. But I do not buy."

Addie said halfheartedly, "What does he do for a living?"

"As to this—I would not wish to soil my brains with imagining. Yet you may depend it is nothing so honest as fisticuffing. If I am not mistaken Joe Montheil once relates that he gets barred from the bar as a lawyer. Finish your plate."

•

# 9

On the way back to the Vauban, Kate Barsony stopped at a grocer's to shop. Addie refused to join her, nor did she accept her invitation to dinner. Kate's blatant cheerfulness jarred because of what had brought it about. For the time being at least, Addie was surfeited with her friend. And too, although she was ashamed to admit it, she could not help being envious of the change in Kate's status. Kate was no longer an intruder in her daughter's house. Addie's position remained the same.

It was past four when she let herself into the apartment. No one was at home. She changed her rough-dried clothes and went to the living room. She was too restless to read or sew or listen to the radio. She was too restless to do anything but worry. She worried because Lindsey was not there. Often he had returned from school much earlier, which meant that his absence now had nothing to do with preserving the fiction that he was still employed by the Board of Education. She worried that he might be walking the streets in damp shoes. She worried about whatever it was that had brought him to the office building. She worried about his desolate face, the heartbreaking droop of his shoulders. She worried about the post-midnight invasion of the Montheil-Barsony apartment at the very hour when he had been abroad. And repeatedly she muttered the word, "coincidence," as one who tries to learn a lesson. She worried about the drawings, and knew that if they had forced Lindsey to give up his teaching for fear of their coming to light, the police might well consider them sufficient provocation to violence. Not that she really believed he had inflicted that savage beating. Of course not. But the police would believe it. They would be only too glad to believe it. For she had no Fix to give them as an alternate suspect. Fix, the monster, had dwindled to Felix Watling, a little fat man who looked as if he could not fight a cold. A man of sedentary occupation. A—not a lawyer—Lindsey had called him a——? But wasn't there enough to worry her without bothering her head about his profession? To prove that there was she went through the list all over again.

It was five o'clock. It was six o'clock. It was seven. She prowled the apartment like an abandoned cat. The foyer, her room, the room of Lindsey and Elaine. Where were they? Surely they had never been so late. Could Elaine have chosen this day to desert the sinking ship? And Lindsey *was* a sinking ship. She had caught in that one frightening glimpse a signal of distress clearer than any telegraphed SOS. And she, his mother, had been unable to heed it. Somewhere along the line, she thought, she must have erred. If in his childhood she had tried hard enough to break through his reserve, to win his trust, he might have turned to her now. How many times had she greeted George with, "Lindsey's in one of his touch-me-not moods." How many times had they raised their eyebrows at each other, or maybe laughed, and let it go at that. The sulks, as George called them, always ran their course. Attempts to divert or josh Lindsey out of them did not work. Even George gave that up in mock despair before Lindsey had reached his teens. She? Well—she had not paid much attention one way or the other. Her method had been to act as though she did not notice, and to caution Nanny Lou to do the same. Nanny Lou was so different. There were no dark byways in Nanny Lou's make-up. Had that been the trouble? Had she neglected Lindsey because Nanny Lou was such a satisfying, responsive child? Had she loved Nanny Lou just a little more, just enough to make her son feel robbed? But George had taken the opposite path and Nanny Lou had not felt robbed. I am as bad as Jancsi with her guilt, she thought. All this was long ago. What has it to do with the man he has become—with the beating—the drawings—the police——?

Someone was at the door at last. Lindsey? Elaine? Elaine. The girl's free long-legged stride brought her across the foyer and into the living room. She was laden with brown paper bags and she was short of breath.

She said, "Good evening, Mother Prentice," and looked around the room, and then looked blank. She tossed her hat and coat on a chair and went to dump the bags in the kitchenette. Addie followed her, standing by while she stowed rolls in the breadbox, cans on a shelf, and meat and a packet of frozen vegetables in the refrigerator.

"You must be starved," Elaine said over her shoulder, "but I couldn't help—I was detained. Where's Lindsey gone?"

"He hasn't come home yet."

Elaine turned around, leaving the refrigerator door open. "He hasn't come home? But it's a quarter to eight. How long have you been——?"

"I got in about four."

"Didn't he phone to say——?"

"Not while I was here."

"That's funny."

Not very, Addie thought. She hesitated to speak. It seemed a kind of betrayal to say that she had seen Lindsey.

"I splurged on a steak," Elaine said. "I thought it might do him—might cheer things up—but I guess there's no use starting it until he comes."

Addie said mechanically, "No—better not. He likes it rare."

"Do you mind waiting?"

"Don't give it a thought. I'm not the least bit hungry." Addie closed the gaping refrigerator door. "But maybe you ought to take a little something to keep you going."

"I'm not hungry either. I had lunch late."

In the living room she sank into a chair, kicked off her shoes, and stooped to massage her slim feet.

Addie saw her grimace with pain. "I'll get your slippers," she said.

"Don't bother." But when Addie brought them, Elaine smiled at her. It was not a happy smile, but for a moment it lifted the cool mask she wore. "Thanks. I guess I've been doing too much gallivanting." Abruptly she put an end to small talk. "Any further developments across the hall? The newspapers hardly gave it a play."

Addie wondered how much or how little to tell her. She was given time to decide because Elaine reached for a cigarette and spoke with her face turned away. "The late edition said someone had broken into the Montheil apartment."

Addie said, "Yes," in a stifled voice, and Elaine's head swiveled, presenting a full view of the shadowed gray eyes, the tensed curve of the wide mouth.

"I gathered that the robbery took place in the wee small hours," Elaine said.

"It wasn't exactly a robbery. Nothing was stolen."

"That makes it worse."

Addie did not have to ask what she meant. She said, "Don't

go imagining things. It's coincidence—that's all it is—coincidence."

"Of course."

Addie resented the subtle shading of the ordinary words. If Lindsey's wife had no faith in him, who would? But then she thought, I have no right to criticize her. I'm his mother and even I——

"I wonder what's detaining Lindsey," Elaine said. She might have been introducing an entirely new subject. "School sure keeps late these days."

Addie tasted unaccustomed anger. "Stop it," she said loudly.

Elaine stared at her. "Stop what?"

"You confided in me last night. Why take it all back by pretending to me now? I know he's left off teaching. I'd have to be more of an old fool than I am not to know a lot of things you both tried to spare me——"

Elaine looked nonplused. "I never thought you were any kind of a fool, Mother Prentice." She sounded shy. "The way things are I haven't had as much chance as I'd like to get acquainted with you—but you'll have to believe it wasn't because I didn't want to."

"Oh yes," Addie said, "I know all about that too. You got a job to help out."

Elaine did not deny it. She glanced ruefully at her feet in their shabby mules. "A fine job—modeling fur coats—beautiful ton-heavy fur coats—with time and a half for working late—but I didn't get paid anything extra for tonight because—well —that's another story."

"If you'd told me about the job I could have made things easier for you by taking the household chores off your hands—but no—I sat around like a stick of wood——"

"Lindsey didn't want me to tell you—and he didn't want you to keep house for him. He wanted you to do nothing but sew a fine seam."

"For mercy's sake——!"

"It's beyond me, too," Elaine said. "I suppose it was part of proving to himself that he and not his sister would sustain you in your—now that he was a man."

"What's his sister got to do with it?"

"He was jealous of her—wasn't he? At least that's my impression. In fact—long before I met you I was prepared to dislike you on sight—just from remarks he'd dropped——"

"Does he—does he dislike me?"

"Far from it—the trouble must have started because he wanted to be tops with you. That's why he was so pleased at being appointed supervisor. It meant more money—it meant he could take care of you. And then—and then he had to get into this mess. It exploded too late to stop you from coming—and now he's so ashamed he can hardly bear to face you. Do you see?"

Addie saw.

Elaine took pity on her. "He's a mixed-up guy. I don't know much about what happens in families, myself—because I had no sisters or brothers—or for that matter no mother and father I can remember—but I do know you'd never play favorites—not that he actually said you did but——" It was obvious that her mind barely touched upon what she was saying. It was busy elsewhere. "Did you—did I hear you say he'd stopped teaching? What gave you that idea?"

It was Addie's turn to look nonplused. She could have sworn that Elaine spoke in honesty. If Elaine did not know that Lindsey had quit his job, then maybe it was not so. The detective could have been wrong, or she could have been wrong in her interpretation of his morning call. And if Lindsey still taught, the situation was not so serious as she had allowed herself to believe. He might have been excused from his classes because he had legitimate business to transact; quite separate business from that which had prompted Jancsi's errand. After all, the office building was large, housing many trades and professions. She decided to put it to Elaine. But first she said bluntly, "Do you really mean to leave Lindsey?"

"I wish you'd forget that pretty conversation."

"Well—do you?"

"My threat to leave was bravado," Elaine said. "Big empty bravado. I wish I could go."

Addie said without rancor, "Because of me?"

"You?"

"I heard you say he should never have brought me here. I don't hold it against you. What I'm trying to find out is——" But she could not say what she was trying to find out. It had to come unprompted from Elaine's lips.

Elaine said, "Maybe I did say something like that—only you heard it out of context and jumped to an absolutely wrong conclusion. I meant because we'd uprooted you and were giving you absolutely nothing to substitute for what you'd left behind."

"Then why do you wish you could leave? Is it want of money that keeps you?"

Elaine shook her head. "No—it's something called love." She was embarrassed. "We were as happy as anything until—until this business happened. He was coming out of that shell of his and—oh damn—damn——"

Addie was embarrassed too. But she was satisfied. Lindsey's wife, who loved him, had a right to know everything that concerned him. In an "enough of this nonsense" tone she spoke her piece. She began with the detective and ended with her lunch at Kate's tea-and-coffee emporium. So heavily were the details of the day stamped upon her mind that she left out little of what the detective had said, what Jancsi had said, what Kate had said, and what she herself had said and seen and done.

Elaine listened. Elaine nodded once or twice. The hollows on her cheeks became more pronounced and less attractive.

She seemed to shed weight as she sat there. And when at last she spoke, even her voice was thin. "He's quit all right. Well —that does it."

It was sentence being pronounced upon Addie's hopes. She tried to appeal it. "You mustn't make the same mistake I made." Unconsciously, she paraphrased Kate. "The detective talked to everybody in the hotel—from manager to elevator boy. Just because he called on me and just because I happened to lay eyes on Lindsey doesn't——"

Elaine stopped her. "Let's face it. If that's all there was to it there might be a hundred explanations. But it's backed by too many things to have more than one—things I couldn't register fully because I was tired and depressed and generally sub in all departments. For instance there was the way he'd got so careless of his appearance when he'd been almost finicky about setting the students a good example—and there was the way he stopped being stiff-necked about letting me get a job—and there was that business of the check you gave him for his birthday. Not even his worst enemy could accuse him of being stingy. If he had ten cents he'd insist that I take nine—but he pocketed your check without offering me a penny of it and never mentioned it again. He must have used it for us to live on—so he wouldn't have to tell me his salary wasn't coming in any more. And if ever we needed it—we're going to need it now." Then she said, "I might as well tell you why. I've got to tell somebody and it doesn't seem just the right moment for breathing it into his ear. I went to the doctor today—which is the reason I stayed late—to make up for the time I spent away from the job—plus the time the police took. They came to see me, too——"

"Wait—wait a minute," Addie said.

"Yes—I'm going to have a baby."

"Child—my dear child—that's wonderful!"

Elaine said flatly, "It could have been."

"It will be—you'll see—everything will be all right. You must tell him as soon as he comes in. He'll——" She ended weakly, "He'll be the happiest man in the world."

Elaine lowered her eyes to her wrist watch. She jiggled the watch, then held it to her ear. She muttered, "Wouldn't it be a laugh if he walked out on me?" Her face answered the question. Her face was tragic.

Addie's watch said a quarter to nine. As much to comfort Elaine as to conceal her own dismay, she said, "We could still be barking up the wrong tree. Lindsey could still be getting his salary. Maybe the five hundred dollars went for—for hush money."

"No. Joe had been touching him all right—which was why we're in such straitened circumstances—but I doubt if Lindsey would have been misguided enough to let him know he'd had a windfall. And even if he had—it was hush money that didn't hush—or there wouldn't have been any need to kill——"

"Don't say it!" Addie's voice was shrill. "Don't you dare say it—don't you dare think it. Hear?"

"How can I help it?"

"You've got to help it. Listen to me—he was never—as a child he never had more than his quota of fights. He was a strange little button—hard sometimes for me and his father to understand—but never rough." Her voice warmed, recovering its normal pitch. "Mind you—he wasn't a sissy—the other boys had too much respect to pick on him—but while they were busy wrestling and scrapping and getting bloody noses, his nose was in some art book—or he was out painting landscapes—except in the football season—he did love football—and what with his fine build he was mighty——" She held Elaine's attention. She had a feeling that she could hold it indefinitely with tales of Lindsey's childhood, and so hold fear at bay. But her own attention strayed. Her present fear would not lie dormant behind a door constructed of the past.

It crouched, waiting, ready to tear her apart. Lindsey, she thought, why aren't you here where you belong? Please—please—don't do anything foolish. The next time the elevator stops on this floor let it be you. You're going to be a father, Lindsey, and no one with time to give it a proper thought because everything's so confused. Let us hear your key in the lock. Let Elaine—— A rhythmic sound distracted her.

Elaine had moved to the edge of her chair. She was tapping its wooden arm with her fingernails. The quick nervous beat was the heart of the room's silence. Addie's temples began to throb with it. The frantic hand became an enemy. It took restraint to keep from quieting it by force.

Addie said, "You're tired and overwrought. I'll get you a meal——"

The fingers went on tapping.

"Elaine——" She raised her voice. "Elaine——"

The tapping ceased. Elaine said, "I'm sorry—did you say something?" She looked at her watch again.

"Yes—I——" She found that she did have something to say. "This man you referred to as a monster last night—is he the Felix Watling Kate spoke of?"

Elaine nodded.

"The one who came calling here with his wife?"

"Yes. I'd forgotten you'd met him."

"Are you sure he's the one? Doesn't he have a brother or a cousin or some kin of the same name?"

"Not that I know of. Why?"

"I just thought he might. Kate insists the Felix Watling she knows isn't married."

"I wouldn't be surprised if she was right." Elaine moved restlessly, but at least she did not resume the tapping. She went on without interest, "But he's the same one all right. People like him don't have relations. They crawl full grown from the mud."

Addie wailed, "But he's so fat and flabby."

Elaine reacted to that. She stopped looking remote and looked as though she were suddenly confronted by a lunatic. She said, "There's no point in waiting dinner any longer. It will do us both good to eat." She stood up. To Addie, her startled eyes said, Do I have to put up with this, too?

Addie said, "I haven't lost my wits. I'm only trying to get at the root of the matter and I'd somehow pinned my hopes on Fix—Felix Watling. But even if Joe was slight—he was the wiry kind—and the man I met could never have got the best of him in a fight."

"Oh." Elaine sat down again. She retired into another silence. Warily, Addie watched her hands. Her caught breath was released in a great sigh when Elaine spoke.

"You might have something there, Mother Prentice—except there's one thing I can't get around. I'm not worried about Watling's lack of muscle. He's not the type who does his own dirty work. It would be quite simple for him to hire someone to do it for him. But he wouldn't arrange to have Joe Montheil killed. Joe was useful to him."

"In what way?"

"Some venture they were in together. A big venture according to both of them. I haven't a clue as to what it was."

"Does Lindsey know?"

"I suppose so. He must—because they were holding the drawings over his head to bring him into the fold. Joe's blackmail was just a side line. But although I've begged and threatened and made scenes he won't tell me what it's all about."

"Do you know what Felix Watling did for a living before he went into this—this venture? That might give us some——"

"Probably all sorts of petty racketeering. His title seems to have a two-way stretch."

"His title——?"

"One of the detectives who came to see me today said that

he was a disbarred lawyer. Aside from being short for Felix—Fix is underworld slang for lawyers."

"You told the detectives about him?"

"Of course. I wanted them to know the sort of company Joe kept. Not that I could tell them much—and not that they got at all excited when I brought his name into it."

"Oh." Then Addie said, "But it wasn't a lawyer."

"What wasn't?"

"What Lindsey said when he introduced him to me—his profession—only I can't seem to recall——"

Elaine said too patiently, "Lindsey introduced him as a publisher—out of respect to you. I guess he thought that a character like that in his living room required some sort of justification." Her mouth twisted. "Lindsey has slightly confused but very strict ideas of propriety."

"Do you know where Fix lives?"

"Under a rock of course." She raised her hands and pressed them to her forehead.

Addie said compassionately, "Maybe Lindsey left a note for you. Did you——?"

Elaine was out of her chair, out of the room. While she was gone, Addie almost succeeded in convincing herself that she had seen a note on Elaine's dressing table. She even managed to visualize the envelope. It was the kind Lindsey had used for his letters home, white and square, and crammed with a reassuring explanation of why he had been detained. When she heard Elaine's voice at the telephone in the foyer, the vision of the envelope vanished.

"Hello—Desk? . . . I didn't ask for my mail when I came in—would you mind looking to see if there's a note from—if there's anything in my box? . . . Thanks. . . . No? . . . Never mind—I'll get the others in the morning."

She came back but did not sit down. She continued on to the kitchenette, saying as she passed Addie, "That's that."

Addie heard dishes rattling. Then there was silence. She bent over the watch that George had given her, and for the first time its face seemed smug, its hands uncaring. She found Elaine standing idle on the little patch of linoleum.

Elaine said dully, "It's after ten—and I can't even think of anywhere he might be. We dropped all our friends as soon as Joe started his squeeze. Lindsey wouldn't accept invitations he couldn't return."

"That's like Lindsey," Addie said, not knowing what she said, concerned only with what she must say. "Elaine—I don't —I hate to put notions into your head—but it does happen. He might—he might have been injured—not seriously—but enough so that they'd take him to a hospital. I've read that in accident cases—no matter how slight—they always insist on——"

For a moment Lindsey was mirrored in Elaine's eyes, a maimed inert Lindsey. Slowly she shook her head. "We'd have been notified. He carries identi——"

"All the same shouldn't we just call the police and——"

"The police!"

"Why not?" But as soon as it was out she knew why not. Her mind raced away with it. The police was no longer a protective body that could be appealed to in time of emergency. It became all too clear to her. The police had picked Lindsey up. They had seated him on a hard chair beneath harder lights. They were denying him food and drink. Their voices were hammering piercing words into his head. They were punctuating the words with blows. Confess, they shouted. Confess! The unwinding reels of her imagination were fed by a hodgepodge of newspaper and screen stories. She did not have to explain them to Elaine. Elaine seemed to be watching them with her. Elaine raised a clenched hand as though she were performing a ritual of exorcism.

Addie's voice was old and rusty. "We've got to find out. I'll phone——"

"No. If they haven't arrested him you'll only put ideas—wait—I've thought of something. He was with Jancsi in that office building. It's mad to think he wasn't. I'm going to see if she's home."

"Jancsi won't tell you anything. She——"

"Oh yes she will," Elaine said with cold assurance.

# 10

Elaine did not stop to put on her shoes. Her mules clicked against her heels as she cut across the foyer. At the door she turned impatiently to address her shadow. "Please don't come with me. I'll do better without an audience. Besides—Lindsey just might——"

She did not end the sentence. She switched on the overhead light, spun around, and pulled the door wide.

The man who had knocked loomed large and ominous. This, Addie thought foolishly, must be Fix. This is how he really looks; the forward head, the thick powerful shoulders, the hand concealed in the pocket of the dark overcoat.

But the hidden hand emerged, holding nothing more sinister than a leather folder, which was flipped open to show printing beneath a face. And the voice that accompanied the gesture had nothing in it of the underworld as portrayed by Hollywood.

"Sorry to call so late," the mild voice said, "I'd like to see Mr. Lindsey Prentice."

"So would I," Elaine muttered.

"Pardon?"

Elaine watched him stow his credentials away. She straightened her tall graceful body, and when she spoke again it was in the light cool tones of everyday. "My husband isn't in. I'll be glad to take a message for him."

"I'm not in such a hurry I couldn't wait for him awhile." His mildness was deceptive, Addie thought. It reminded her of an adage often quoted by George. *There are more ways of killing a cow than slitting its throat.* Evidently, this latest police emissary lived by that adage.

Both she and Elaine stepped aside to let him enter, knowing he would have entered anyway. And anyway, she thought with lifting heart, his intrusion must mean that Lindsey is still at large. And that's something to be thankful for.

The man missed little as he crossed the foyer. He glanced into the bedrooms. He opened the bathroom door and backed away as though he had mistaken it for their destination. And in the living room he strolled toward the kitchenette to survey with an assumption of absent-mindedness its small interior. But Addie might have been an absorbing book for the way he settled his eyes upon her.

"Are you this young lady's mother?"

"She's as close to me as if I were—but Mr. Lindsey Prentice is my born son." She found that she could still say it with pride. She met his eyes coldly. "I noticed you've been taking a good look around. Do you think we lied when we said he was out?"

He showed rabbity teeth. "Why no, ma'am. I guess maybe I was looking to see if a neighbor had dropped in. I wouldn't want any gossip spread about you entertaining cops." He turned to Elaine. "What time do you expect your husband?"

Elaine said slowly, "That depends—on whether he's gone to a movie or dropped in to see friends."

"Didn't he say?"

"No."

His lips were thick and not very skillfully shaped. But the smile he gave Elaine was skillful, notwithstanding the rabbit's teeth. "Most wives keep tabs."

"They probably haven't much else to do," Elaine said.

"Did he tell you he might go to a movie or drop in on friends?"

"I didn't ask."

"What's the matter? Aren't you talking to each other?"

"I haven't seen him since breakfast," Elaine said. "I'm a working girl. Tonight I worked late because two detectives came to question me this afternoon—and the atmosphere after they left made me feel it would be wise for me to repay my employer for the inroads upon his time." Her voice took on just the right tinge of exasperation. "It never occurred to me that I'd be questioned further."

Addie gave her more than a passing mark. She heard the intruder say with creditable surprise, "But I didn't come to question you," and she thought it was time for her to take the onus from Elaine. She did her best to imitate the girl's aplomb. "Well—if you came to question my son you've seen for yourself that he's not here. I like to be as hospitable as the next but my daughter has to rise pretty early in the morning——"

"So does your son, ma'am. Doesn't he?"

That shook them both. They dared not look at each other.

He went on equably, "That's why I'm hoping he won't stay out too late. You sure you got no idea where he is?"

"Yes," Elaine said.

"Yes what?"

"Yes I'm sure I have no idea where he is. That's what you asked—isn't it?"

Neither of them had invited him to sit down. He did so now, settling his large frame with a maddening air of permanence.

"Would you like a cushion?" Elaine said.

His eyes were brown and flat, as though they had been painted on to his face without highlights. "No thanks. I'm fine."

Elaine's mules clicked angrily as she strode over to the mock fireplace. But she lit a cigarette with steady hand.

Addie thought with admiration, Could I have been like that when I was her age? If put to the test could I have exercised such self-control? Now, white hair ruffled by a fidgety hand, the crumpled skin of her cheeks flushed, she felt like an awkward schoolgirl in the presence of authority. And so she too sat down.

"How about you, ma'am?" he said. "Didn't your son confide in you either? Sometimes they'll tell their mamas more than they'll tell their wives."

"I haven't spoken to him today. I left right after the detective questioned *me* this morning." She put a sharp point on it, but his surface was too smooth or too tough to be penetrated.

"You must have had something pretty important to do—assuming you're not a working girl too. The rain sure came down heavy this morning."

The wide nervous gape of her jaws was a gift from heaven. She made the most of it. "I've got something pretty important to do this minute—and that's sleep."

"I'm real disappointed in you," he said. "You don't look like the kind of mama would dream of sleeping unless her boy was safe at home—not without he'd told her what he was up to."

The schoolgirl in Addie took over. "How many detectives do they have on this case anyway?"

"As many as they think are needed."

"Then why don't they compare notes so's they won't all have

to go over the same line of country? I've been questioned—my daughter's been questioned—and I should think if they had it in mind to hound my son they'd have attended to it last night when he was here."

"Was he here all last night?"

Distressed, she thought, Oh Lord—I purely handed him that on a platter. She said steadily, "He certainly was," and her heart cried fiercely, I'll go on lying if I have to hang for it.

He said, "You and the young lady—you'd both be willing to take oath he was—supposing it should come up?"

Elaine left the fireplace. "Why should it come up?" She sounded relaxed, but there was a curious awkwardness in the way she lowered herself into a chair.

His voice was sad. "I'm afraid that won't do. I'd like a straight answer——"

"That goes for me, too," Elaine said. "So it seems we've reached an impasse. But of course it doesn't matter since you aren't here to question me."

"I guess you've got me. I can't make you——"

"No—you can't," Elaine said.

"Only thing is—you aren't helping your husband any."

"Why should he need help?"

He said reprovingly, "You know better than that. You know I wouldn't be here if he didn't need help."

"You don't look like a rescue squad to me," Elaine said. "And what's more you're overdoing the mysterious-sleuth act."

His easy manner changed perceptibly. "Come again?"

"My mother and I have read the papers. They don't say much—but they do say that Joe Montheil died under suspicious circumstances—and they do say that someone unlawfully entered the Montheil apartment after midnight for reasons as yet unknown. Aside from that, my mother—who was in at the death so to speak—and who learned of the other business before the reporters did—has managed to pick up a little information on her own——"

He was sitting well forward, his powerful neck craned. But at her next words he slouched back, resuming his original manner.

"For instance," Elaine said, "my mother heard it straight from the widow's mouth—said widow being one Jancsi Montheil—that she saw fit to serve up my husband to the police as a prime suspect."

"Well—what do you know about that!"

"Your innocence is charming. You haven't heard a thing about that, I'm sure."

"Oh I wouldn't say that."

"No—you wouldn't say anything very much—and while your reticence is charming too it doesn't get us anywhere. Shall we start again?"

"Seems like we're finished—unless you've something to add to the widow Montheil's story."

"I suggest you consult your co-workers. I told them my all this afternoon."

"You're sure you've nothing to add?"

"No—have you?"

He got out of the chair. He looked down at her and said, "Lady—if you'll pardon me being a little personal—you're too easy on the eye to be so sharp."

"Are you leaving?" Elaine said.

"I'm leaving here. I might hang around the lobby in case your husband decides that home is best." His voice contained an insulting doubt.

Addie missed the byplay. She cleared her throat because suddenly she did not want him to leave; not until she had asked what was being done about Felix Watling. Elaine had brought Watling to the attention of the detectives who called at her place of business. But it would not hurt to hammer home her idea that while not physically capable of murder he might have hired someone to do the job.

She gave another preliminary cough. She said, "You don't have to wait in the lobby. You listen to me——"

The ringing telephone silenced her. She and the great hulk and Elaine tangled with each other. The hulk won. None too gently he shoved them out of his way. "Where is it?" he said.

Elaine shouted, "This is my house. You have no right——"

That checked him. He even smiled. "Excuse. I've got a bad habit. Whenever I hear a phone I think it's for me."

"Get out of my way," Elaine said desperately. "It will stop ringing. Mother—hurry——!"

Addie was closest to the foyer. She made goal and lifted the receiver from the hook. She got out a strangled, "Hello," before Elaine reached her side, and then she shook her head, wishing she could have spared Elaine the disappointment so patent upon her face.

She said tonelessly, "Yes, Kate, it's Addie," and had to hold the receiver well away from her ear to protect the sensitive membrane. Kate Barsony's hoarse voice poured into the foyer in a loud ungoverned rush.

"Addie—I know it is criminal that I arouse you but I am beside me and I can stand it alone no longer. I tell you I am out of my head for Jancsi. Not since we last looked on her has she set foot over this threshold—and that was more than ten hours ago. If affairs were normally I would not give this a thought—but you saw how crazy she behaves. Before I call you I have perused through the Red Book under hospitals and I am now far down the alphabet—but each and every one of them assures me her description has not been brought there—not even the one in Brooklyn. Addie—advise me what I am to do. In my shoes would you call again the police or do you think I make mountains from a pimple? Why do you not speak? Say me something——"

Addie said, "I—I don't know what to say. Hold on a minute."

The hulk was standing close behind her. He said, "I could hear it wasn't your son—and if it wasn't I guess it's got nothing to do with me. I'll be running along."

"Just a minute—maybe it has something to do with you. Mrs. Barsony's on the phone. Her daughter, Jancsi, has been away all day and she's frightened because the girl has had a bad shock. She has no idea where——"

"The way you people lose sight of your nearest and dearest," he said. His flat eyes were unreadable. "Has she called the police?"

"Not yet. She wants my advice—and since you represent them——"

"Sure," he said, "I'll pass the information along. One way or the other it's bound to be police business."

"One way or the other?"

He shrugged. "How would you figure it? There's your son—and there's the widow Montheil—both unaccounted for. I got too much respect for this poor lady here"—he jerked a large spatulate thumb at Elaine—"to draw any diagrams—but she being so sharp she won't need me to lay it out for her."

A distinct white ridge outlined Elaine's lips and nostrils. She said, "What's your name?"

Addie was brushed by fleeting astonishment that so much contempt could be packed into such a simple question. Not that she did not second it. After a lifetime as a decent citizen she suddenly found herself in complete accord with that segment of the public which despised and flouted the forces of law and order.

"My name? Same as it was on my credentials. Leo—Sergeant Leo. You wouldn't want to recommend me for a promotion, would you? I haven't done a thing but carry out orders. Sleep well, ladies."

The door closed quietly behind him, but the stamp of his presence clung to the foyer, to Elaine, white-lipped and silent, to Addie as she turned once more to the crackling telephone.

"Kate . . . Yes . . . I know—I'm sorry—I couldn't help . . . Kate—let me . . . I've told the police about Jancsi . . . No—no I don't think it's serious but it can't hurt to have them know . . . Yes—I'm sure she's all right . . . I . . . Yes—phone me again if she . . . No—I can't leave here right now but . . . Yes—if I can." She put the receiver back on its hook.

She said to Elaine, "The poor thing's so worried."

# 11

Addie heated milk and buttered some bread. She called Elaine and coaxed her to take nourishment, insisting that it was the sensible thing to do.

The milk did not act upon either of them as a soporific. Elaine's gray eyes held no suggestion of sleep as she announced stonily that she was going to bed. "Now that it's every man for himself," she said, "I'd better not turn up at work looking like a hag. I need to hold on to my job for as long as I can." It was her first reference, oblique or direct, to the intelligence concerning Jancsi.

Addie, who had been waiting for an opening, said, "Don't try to make me believe you have so little faith. Why—it was fine the way you gave that sergeant his comeuppance——"

"I've got my pride," Elaine said. "Not that it's going to be much company for me in the lean years ahead."

"What kind of talk is that? You look here—wherever Jancsi is she's not with Lindsey."

Elaine damned her with faint praise. "You mean well, Mother Prentice."

The demoted Addie, who had held the superior rank of "Mother" while the detective was there, said simply, "I could just shake you."

"If you hit me with a piano I wouldn't feel it," Elaine said.

"Answer me this—did it ever seem to you that they had the slightest interest in each other?"

"I've been a dope in more ways than one."

Addie ignored it. "No—it didn't—and why? Because it isn't true—that's why. If there had been anything of that sort you'd have known it right off the bat—and don't tell me you wouldn't. You're far and away too smart to be taken in."

"Sharp is the word our big friend used," Elaine said.

"He's no friend of mine."

"Jancsi is very beautiful," Elaine said, as though she were reading from a dull textbook.

"No more beautiful than you." Both might have forgotten that a man named Montheil had ever existed, or that his sudden death bore upon their present situation.

"Thanks," Elaine said. She carried the dishes and saucepan to the sink and washed them with mechanical efficiency. "Don't bother to dry—let them drain. Good night. It behooves me to keep what looks I've got since modeling's the only thing I know. Maybe Lane Bryant will take me on when——"

"Child—he's not with Jancsi. I saw him leave that office building alone."

"He's not here," Elaine said. She headed for her bedroom.

Addie could not refute that exit line. She called out, "Do you mind being alone for a little while?"

"Ha-ha," Elaine said. "In parenthesis."

"I mean——" Addie cursed herself for being tactless. "I thought I'd stop in and see how Kate Barsony's doing. I promised I would if——"

"Help yourself," Elaine said. She went into her bedroom and closed the door.

Addie crossed the hall with no zest for this latest tax upon her depleted resources. Kate flew to answer her knock. Kate was a gaunt and ancient bird who croaked, "Addie—you?"

"She hasn't come home yet?"

"Perhaps not forever. It is a judgment upon me." She flapped the wings of her flowing violet robe. "Enter. At least it is to be thankful you are not another reporter from the newspapers. One comes who says he writes a feature story about Joe Montheil. He demands pictures of the departed and of my Jancsi too—but I rid myself by yelling I am a communist and if he does not depart I will take bombs from my bosom to blow him up."

Addie followed her to the living room. Its unnatural tidiness was marred only by some black garments thrown upon the sofa.

Kate said in the exhaling of one breath, "I am unable to sit still so I order the entire establishment from head to toes and you would be amazed what this maid from the hotel overlooks under the bed and in the corners but no hard feelings for tomorrow when she comes she will find some gifts as I have also made neat the closets." She paused, but only for a moment. "Addie—you called the police for me?"

"There was a detective in my apartment. He said he'd pass the word along."

Kate seemed to accept the detective's presence as one accepts exits and entrances in a dream. "He perhaps ventured an opinion?"

Addie said grimly, "Just that he believed her to be safe."

The grimness too was lost. "Could I but believe this also."

"You mustn't believe anything else." She could still find a little room in her burdened heart for Kate's pain. What she could not do was give voice to her own.

Kate begged her to sit down, sweeping the black garments off the sofa. "I am remaking for the funeral," she explained. "Naturally there is Jancsi to consult—but meanwhile I think it is wasteful to purchase new costumes merely for one occasion and I commence to sew while I await her. I reason she will agree not to buy new since she is not her best in black—for she is so small it makes her to disappear——" She stopped. "Oh Addie—you hear what I speak? Disappear I say."

"Now, Kate——"

"You recall how you and I sit so foolish in the park and discuss our troubles?"

Addie nodded.

"Such troubles I would have back," Kate said. "It shows you. Addie—I have been stretching every brain in my head and yet I cannot fathom where she is. I have brought to the telephone all the possibles in her addresses book but they sound only surprised when I ask, 'Is Jancsi with you?' Addie—do not be so temporary. Sit."

But she herself did not sit. She roamed the room, clutching a black dress to her bosom. Addie had to trail after her to make herself heard.

"I can't stay very long, Kate. Elaine is—she isn't well—and —and Lindsey's been detained."

"I am sorry." Kate was at the window. Her stance made of the dark courtyard a lighted avenue down which Jancsi might walk at any moment.

Addie said to her back, "I wish there was something I could do." It was a blanket statement covering both of them.

Kate wheeled. "I also wish. Addie—do you consider that I have been too forward spoken with Jancsi—that I have enraged her to where she can no longer tolerate my company? I am often an exploding woman with no sense to control. I——"

"Kate—Jancsi understands that whatever you've said or done is because you love her."

Apparently, Kate did not hear. She was peering again into the dark courtyard.

"Kate—I wasn't going to tell you but—you're not the only one who's worried sick. Lindsey hasn't come home either—and we just don't know what to——"

Kate turned, her expression so indrawn that it was impossible to tell whether or not she had heard. Addie was startled to hear her say with hysterical brightness, "This settles it. Addie—I am mad to hold you here. Friendship is friendship but there is also to observe limits. We will bid good night——"

"I don't like to leave you. Are you sure——?"

"One thing I am sure. I push on my clothes and I march myself to the station house." As she talked she was marching Addie to the door. "I will discover its address in the telephone book. It is open all the night—no? It is not an organization to shut up at eight hours like a respectable business. So I go there and I sit there until something happens—even should I have to see the king of all policemen. And if while I am away Jancsi arrives she employs her key and nothing is lost."

Bewildered, Addie found herself in the hall, the heat of Kate's fingers still upon her arm. She plodded back to the Prentice apartment.

When she had let herself in, she listened with caught breath for a male voice, a cough, a step, anything that would point to the wanderer's return. She even did a thing she would have thought impossible a few days ago. She opened the door that Elaine had closed, and looked inside. The foyer's light gave her Elaine's slim shape beneath the covers. The empty white pillow beside her head was the largest object in the room. She knew that Elaine was awake and aware of her standing there at the door, although she neither stirred nor spoke.

If Elaine could go to bed, she supposed she could. It was not as though she had a practical alternative, unless to follow Kate to the police station was practical. She went into her own room and started to remove her dress. She visualized the picture she and Kate would present; two ridiculous old ladies perched on a hard bench, addressed by a composite of the sandy and the dark and the large detective. The composite said, "What can I do for you, ladies?" and she and Kate chorused, "We are neighbors who have lost our children. Please will you find them and bring them home?"

A little yelp of laughter escaped her and she covered her mouth with her hand. I'd better get to bed—and fast, she thought.

She had not dared to expect sleep. Her tired eyes seemed stretched to such an unnatural size that the stiff hot lids no longer fit them. And as she lay, trying to compose herself, her body began to itch. For no reason at all, she told herself miserably. The hotel is clean. I can at least say that for it. Yet, no sooner had she scratched one place when the itch broke out in another. And anyway it seemed to spring from deep beneath the skin and scratching did not reach it. And why was she fussing so when there were those who would give anything to lie in a bed. Lindsey—Lindsey—Kate. Kate—a thin old lady upright on a hard bench—a pillow to put between Kate's meager upholstery and the hard hard bench—the empty wasted pillow in Elaine's—poor Elaine—and the blessed unborn——

Next it was morning, and the fitful dreams she had dreamed were gone, leaving behind no memory, but only renewed anxiety and an increased heaviness of limb and spirit. Not replenished by that haunted sleep, Addie arose. She raised the window shade and glimpsed the sun, and such was her state that she disputed its right to shine. Her watch said, "Seven-thirty." Her heart said, "Dark of night."

By the time she had bathed and dressed she smelled coffee and found Elaine drinking it in the living room. Drinking it black. Eating nothing.

"I didn't expect you'd be up so early," Elaine said, "what with one thing and another." She fetched cream and sugar and a second cup. "I'm sorry I can't stop to get you anything more."

"Let me get *you* something."

Elaine shook her head.

"But now more than ever you need food——" At Elaine's rebellious expression she changed her theme. "How can you work on an empty stomach—if you're really going to work?"

"Of course I'm going."

"Did you sleep?"

Elaine lied away the violet shadows beneath her eyes. "Like a—like a cat."

"I can imagine," Addie said. "Couldn't I call your employer and——?"

"You could if you wanted to watch me go mad—sitting around doing nothing."

Addie supposed she was right. She said no more about it. They finished the coffee in silence, Addie without the energy to express her thoughts, Elaine without the desire.

But on the verge of leaving the apartment, Elaine came back and said, "I'll give you my number. They don't like us to receive calls but—well—in case you should want to——"

"I'll call. The minute there's news I'll call," Addie said. "You can be sure of that."

Elaine bent and kissed her cheek and said in a strangled voice, "I wish you had something to do, too—to take your mind off——"

"I'll be all right," Addie said, her own voice choked. "I'll find something to do. You take care. Hear?"

As soon as Elaine had gone, Addie turned on the radio and

hunted the dial for a news program. She heard plenty of news but none of it dealt with the Montheil murder. Not important enough, she thought. What's important about a man being killed in this city? Nothing to make them beat the drums unless the man himself was important. She went to the door to see if Lindsey's *Times* had come. It was not there. Perhaps Elaine had picked it up on the way out. The *Times* was a fine paper. Did—did murderers read the *Times?*

She attended to the coffeepot and the cups and saucers, a duty outside the sphere of the hotel maid. It consumed no more than minutes. She let a few more pass before she went to the telephone. She dared not call the police for news of Lindsey. If—if it all turned out to be a mistake, her inquiry would only sharpen their interest in him. She called the Montheil apartment. That did not take very long, no longer than for the operator downstairs to ring the required number of times and announce triumphantly that there was no answer.

Addie dismissed the thought that Kate was still glued to a bench in the police station. Kate, that energetic, indomitable woman, had simply started her day early and was away on some errand. Jancsi? She refused to think about Jancsi.

She sat at the telephone table in the foyer, staring at the cold instrument. She leaped as footsteps halted at the door.

The tumbler of the lock clicked, and the hotel maid entered. She saw Addie and said apologetically, "I didn't know anyone was home. I would've knocked if——"

"That—that's all right."

"Why—Mrs. Prentice—you're white as a sheet. I don't wonder I scared you—what with all the goings on in this place." She was a wispy young woman whose strength seemed centered in her aggressively waved blond hair. On one thin arm she carried a pail crammed with cloths, a brush, and a dustpan. The other strained around a brown paper parcel and what looked like a stack of lurid magazines. She set the pail down with a clatter and placed the other burden beside it. "I didn't bring my mop. It ain't my day for mopping," she said. "You been vacuumed this week?"

"I don't—I guess so."

"Well—it don't look it. I'll speak to Micky. Micky was supposed to do it. Go right ahead."

"Go ahead?"

"You sitting at the phone—I thought maybe you was getting ready to call somebody when I came in."

"I've finished calling."

"Oh." She did not start to work. She smoothed the unsmoothable hair with a hand tipped by cracked nail polish. Her pale protruding eyes were on the bundle at her feet. She said conspiratorily, "I just been there."

Addie said through her private mist, "Where?"

"Acrost the hall—where Mr. Montheil got his. Is it true he died in your arms after whispering to you who it was?"

Addie shook her head. She could not speak.

The maid was disappointed. "Well—that's what they're saying." She brightened. "Nobody was home while I cleaned—and there wasn't much cleaning to do either—Mr. Montheil must have been the messy one and not the Hungarian lady or the young missus like I always thought. The Hungarian lady left that bundle and the comic books for me." She knelt and began to dust the rungs of Addie's chair. "Lots of times she gives me stuff. She's okay—better than some I could mention who speak good English. The bundle's got a brocaded dress in it—old-fashioned but the material's swell—and a knitted stole which is stylish again—and a few other odds and ends I can use. The comic books is for my kids. They keep buying or swapping them in school all the time. They'll have a field day with these. Just look how nice and clean. Don't seem they've hardly been touched." She plucked one from the pile and handed it to Addie.

Addie took it because she could not bear to rebuff anyone. She turned the pages idly, pretending interest. All at once she stopped pretending. The blood had risen to her cheeks before she stooped for the rest of the books.

The maid, who had progressed from chair rungs to table top, said cordially, "Help yourself."

Holding the books, Addie said, "Have you looked at these?"

"Not yet. I didn't get the chance."

Addie made a heroic effort. "I'll tell you," she said. "It happens I'm calling on a sick child today. I've got to take her something and it's been kind of hard to figure out just what—but these would fill the bill all right. If you'd be kind enough to sell them to me I'd give you more than they're worth. I figured to spend a few dollars anyway."

The maid eyed her with an assumption of shrewdness. "Sure—I know how it is, Mrs. Prentice. They pass the time—I even read them myself. I guess a couple of dollars is more than my kids would get—and they'll never know the difference. Glad to oblige." She picked up her pail. "The kitchenette's due for a scrub. That's where I'll be if you want me."

"Well—thank you. I'll fetch my purse." Addie carried the books to her bedroom. Safe within its close walls she sat on the bed and waited for her nausea to pass.

Kate didn't realize, she thought sickly. She couldn't have so much as glanced at them. In her bout of putting things to rights last night she came across them and set them aside for the maid's children. Children——! Addie closed her eyes because the barren little room was spinning. To place such fare within the reach of children——! She saw herself going to the closet to get a blanket for Joe; saw herself ducking as the pile of comic books toppled, just missing her head. She could not duck their impact now, nor had she time to nurse the blow they dealt her. She must stir herself. She must catch and pin down the flying thoughts that made a buzzing hive of her head.

The room had settled when she opened her eyes. The books sprawled out upon the bed where she had dropped them. She started to restack them, using her fingers gingerly, as though contact with the paper would contaminate. I'll hide them away —take them to the incinerator as soon as the coast is clear. What——? One of the books, as luridly covered as the rest, was different inside. Its contents slid out as she handled it. Not printed matter but a sheaf of onionskin; a carbon copy of someone's penmanship. The top sheet was a letter.

"Pal Fix," she read. "This is kind of a rough dummy. The idea came to me just like that and I've got a million more. So how's about adding me to the staff? I always had a secret yen to be a writer. It means I get a bigger cut but high-class stuff like this don't grow on trees. No hard feelings if you turn it down. I can find a place to peddle it. Of course I'll take my boy along with me. Some team, eh? No stopping us."

The letter was signed, "Joe." The rest of the dummy consisted of graphic captions beneath large blank spaces. And on the last page was scrawled, "I got news for you. The sooner we ditch 'Spheres' as a front the healthier. I discovered there is a 'Spheres.' They publish textbooks and could spell trouble if they got wind of our setup. Boy—you sure need me in your business. How's about it?"

Addie placed the dummy in the center of the printed books. She stowed the lot in her third bureau drawer and covered it with her pristine underwear. She closed the drawer with such force that some of the articles on the bureau, mementos of a happier day, toppled over. She righted them absently. Then she went to the kitchenette, paid the maid, and announced that she was going out.

"Well—it's a nice day," the maid said. "Real warm for a change."

But Addie put on her winter coat because she did not feel warm. As she left the apartment, Elaine's parting words rang through her head. "I wish you had something to do—to take your mind off——" Well, she had something to do. It might not take her mind off, but she had something to do all right.

# 12

She saw the dark detective in the lobby of the Vauban. Minus his sandy partner he stood at the desk, and she hesitated and then shook her head. Even if his back had not been turned to her, even if he had called her name, she would not have allowed herself to be delayed. She was off to accomplish a job that should have been his. Until she had built up a concrete case to present, let him and his stew in their black ignorance.

Grudging the time it took, yet under strong compulsion, she stopped on her way to buy a *Times* and a tabloid. She took them into a drugstore and left her token order of a coke untouched while she scanned them. The *Times* carried the usual headlines of remote minor wars, neither remote nor minor enough, of peace talks, and of Senate investigations. The Montheil tragedy was confined to a single column rehashing the findings of yesterday, and closing with what seemed an afterthought to the effect that Lindsey Prentice, former schoolteacher, was wanted by the police for questioning.

"Former schoolteacher" was bad news to her. It corroborated what she had tried to disbelieve, for she could not doubt the integrity of the *Times*. But she took a modicum of comfort from the words, "Wanted for questioning." He had not been arrested. That was a straw to clutch at. And as for the police wanting him, so did she. So did Elaine. And if it was humanly possible, she meant to find him.

The tabloid's headlines were devoted to another murder, of the type most certain to whet its public's appetite. For three double-page spreads was set forth in pictures and text the gruesome details of an unidentified male body, decapitated and decomposed, which had been washed ashore from Long Island's Great South Bay. Why bother with the simple case of violence which had purportedly ended Joe Montheil's life when there was this to feed upon?

She found Joe on the eighth page. True that he had been given more space than was granted by the *Times*. But the extra wordage took the form of hints and supposition. Were there political motives behind Montheil's demise? Had this dashing young man been a card-carrying communist? When the eager reporter tired of the game he switched to Joe's widow. She was beautiful, he stated. She was extremely popular with the opposite sex. She was Hungarian by birth. And both she and Lindsey Prentice, who had been a boon companion of the dead man, and whom the police sought, had disappeared. Graciously the reporter allowed his readers to draw their own conclusions.

Addie drew blood from her lower lip as she fought for composure. Praying that Elaine would not see the tabloid, she shed both papers and quit the drugstore.

She was not conscious of the day's sunny promise, or of being jostled by people who had found reason or excuse to take advantage of it. She hurried on, only vaguely aware that her suddenly unseasonable coat had become another weight to support. What further thought she spent upon the weather was to compare it to the rain of yesterday, to wish she were out in yesterday's rain, with Jancsi's little figure leading the way. If she had yesterday to live again, she and Kate could run to shorten the distance between themselves and Jancsi. And then, at least, Jancsi would not be missing, and Elaine would be free of that added pain which to the young was the worst pain of all. And if it were yesterday she would have hastened to Lindsey when she saw him and persuaded him to come home and——

She entered the office building and went straight to the wall directory. Her memory had been true. It was there. Spheres Publishing Company was there. And on a line with it she saw and correctly deciphered the numerals, "seventeen" and "forty-two."

Some of the elevators were express, some local. She chose one that would stop at the right floor, and to its operator she said in a loud defiant voice, "Seventeen, please."

During the ascent, her lips moved in silent rehearsal. I wish to speak to Mr. Felix Watling . . . No—I haven't an appointment but he'll see me . . . Tell him Mrs. Prentice is here on important business. But no sooner had she got it letter-perfect when it occurred to her that a variation might be necessary. You say he's not in? What time do you expect him? . . . I see . . . Well—give me his home address, please . . . She prepared, too, for the contingency of refusal. Mr. Watling won't thank you for your attitude. You'll learn that it's very much to his advantage to——

The elevator had made one of its stops. A long stop. The straggle of passengers was shuffling its feet, and the operator said in an injured voice, "Who gave me 'seventeen'? Did they change their minds or what?"

Stiffly, Addie excused herself. With the sensation of being imprisoned in the sort of dream where an essential article of attire is lacking, she stepped out.

She wandered down several corridors, pausing to read the legends upon the doors. The door she wanted was half open, and what she glimpsed within caused her to draw a sobbing breath. It presented a contingency for which she had not prepared.

In stark dismay she crossed the threshold. Before it had been dismantled, the space in which she stood had probably been used as a reception room. Now, the only piece of furniture it contained was a metal filing cabinet with gaping empty drawers. The floor was covered by a splotched tarpaulin, and on it stood two redolent buckets of paint, an overturned wastebasket, a heap of rags, and a telephone.

A door led to an inner office. She started toward it with hardly enough hope left to give her impetus. But it was not her fingers that turned the knob. She saw it move even before she saw the menacing silhouette on the frosted upper panel of the door.

Up to that moment she had heard no sound to warn her of another's presence. Don't get panicky, she told herself. It's only a workman. And if it isn't? If it's Fix? I came to see him, didn't I? She stood her ground. Little and plump and white of face and hair, terribly vulnerable, she stood her ground.

He came out, closing the door behind him. He was not a workman and he was not Fix. He stared down at her from his great height, seeming larger and bulkier than he had been last night. And he greeted her with even softer speech.

"If it isn't Mrs. Prentice."

She backed away, experiencing no relief. She moistened her lips and stammered, "T-then—then the police *are* on to him."

He closed the door that gave on the hall and stood with his back to it. "You referring to your son?"

"No—no—Watling—the man who ran this office."

Playfully he shook a finger at her. "You haven't been trying to keep secrets from us? I don't recall you mentioning Watling last night."

Impatience and indignation strengthened her. "Why should I when I didn't think it would do any good? From the way you all keep after Lindsey—you'd think poor Joe Montheil never knew another soul."

He pushed his hat back on his head and scratched his crop with a rasping sound. "So you decided to do some detecting on your own hook. Old ladies could get into trouble that way."

His playful tone flicked her raw nerves. "Don't try to humor me," she said. "Don't speak of trouble. The trouble my son's in is all I care about. My son's not a coward. He wouldn't run away like this—without a word to—to his wife."

His voice contained the very essence of reason. "He wouldn't —but he did."

She said with dignity, "Maybe I am an old lady—but I'm not exactly in my second childhood and I'll thank you not to treat me like a child. You mark my words—there's another explanation for my son's disappearance."

"I'll be glad to hear it," he said.

"He's with Watling. Somehow—some way—Watling's holding him against his will."

"Now this is real deep stuff. Why should Watling do that?"

"I don't know—that is I——"

"Sure you know," he said genially. "I'm beginning to think you'll be a big help to the police." He looked around the dismantled office as though for counsel. "Why don't we go some place and have a nice talk—some place where we can put our feet up and let our hair down?"

He put a hand into his pocket, the same innocent pocket from which he had produced his credentials last night. And again she thought what she had thought last night. His other hand fell weightily upon her shoulder.

She screamed, "Don't touch me," and the shrewish sound of it echoed in her startled ears.

Instantly he removed the hand. He looked helpless. "Hold it, lady. Habit is all. Comes from making so many arrests." He smiled, showing the rabbit teeth. "You shouldn't have squawked like that. Somebody's liable to think the boss is making passes at his stenographer."

She shook off her unreasoning terror. She nodded in the direction of the inner office. "Didn't you—didn't you find anything in there that would——?"

"Lady—is that fair? Expecting me to get confidential with you when you're holding out on me?"

"I'm not holding out. Most of what I know I discovered this morning." And what would be the use of telling it to you? she thought. You're too smug and arrogant and hateful to believe a word I say.

He had small flat ears, ridiculously out of proportion to the rest of him. She could have sworn she saw them move like the ears of a dog. He said, "What did you discover this morning?"

"No more than what you discovered for yourself—or you wouldn't be here." She laid the facts before him merely to dispute his assumption that she was a harmless idiot. "Watling was setting up to print ugly comic books. He was using this office as a—as a front—and he took the name of Spheres—not knowing it belonged to a respectable publishing firm—but he got scared when he received Joe's letter—and moved before the real Spheres or the police could take any action." She ended bitterly, "Why did you have to leave it till too late?"

"It's not too late. Everything's under control," he said. But his voice was sour. "You sure can add—only it beats me how you came by your figures. Joe's letter for instance——"

"You're wasting time——"

"Whose fault is that? Would I be hung up here talking to you if you'd—well—say if you'd gone to headquarters with your spiel? You didn't think of that—did you?"

"I was going to headquarters after I came here—after I had information they just couldn't afford not to pay heed to. I meant to go and hand it over to them as soon as——"

"You did? Well—like my teacher used to say—we got to be thankful for small mercies."

The smell of the paint in the airless room was making her dizzy, and his reversion to playfulness did not improve the situation. She moved to place her back against the bare wall. She leaned hard. "Why do you stand here doing nothing? Does having everything under control mean that you know his home address—and that you've sent men there to see that he doesn't escape? If you'd only tell me what's happening." She looked at him pleadingly but could read nothing more than insulting tolerance upon his face. She lowered her eyes. Then she stooped and began to go through the few scraps of paper that had spilled from the overturned basket.

"I was fooled that way, too," he said tenderly. "Our bird's cautious. He didn't leave a crumb."

She arose, holding her swimming head. She saw herself as he must see her, an inept amateur. "Then you don't know where he lives?"

"I wouldn't say that. We've got our methods. Thing I'm beginning to wonder is if they're a patch on yours. It's beyond me how you got on to this letter Joe sent. Did he tell you he sent it?"

"How could he? How many times do I have to repeat I only came across the copy of it this morning."

"First I heard of a copy." He glanced at her pocketbook. "You bring it with you?"

"No—I didn't."

Footsteps went by the closed outer door, and again his flat

ears seemed to twitch. "I still think we could find a better place to talk. What say we——"

"I haven't anything else to talk about——"

"Lady—you're modest. You don't know your own strength."

She could take no more of him. He was nothing but a great shell in which rattled a pea-sized brain. "I know one thing—I'm going to the police right now. There must be someone on the force who—who has a little sense."

He did not seem offended. He said heartily, "I call that very sensible. And just to make sure you get there safe and sound I'll be your escort." His hand lifted and started to descend upon her shoulder. But at her recoil he altered its course. He hooked his arm invitingly.

She ignored the arm. She reached the door, opened it, and marched down the hall.

He was behind her as she stepped into the elevator. He was beside her as she found her way through the lobby and out onto the well-peopled sidewalk. There he did take her arm.

"I don't need your help," she said. But his grip was firm and she could not free herself for fear of attracting attention.

"You're not going to tell me a nice lady like you has the address of the Homicide Bureau at her finger tips?"

She remembered that the dark detective had written an address on a piece of paper and left it with her. But where the paper was now, she could not think. She said uncertainly, "I can find the address in the telephone book."

"Why do it the hard way? I got my car handy. I can run you there in two shakes."

She had no answer, so she allowed herself to be steered by him to a parking lot behind the hotel that she and Kate had patronized yesterday. People must feel this way when they're in custody, she thought wryly, except they usually start being arrested at an earlier age. She wondered if passers-by could tell that her companion was a detective. She doubted it. If they received any impression at all it would be the same as hers had been the first time she set eyes upon him. And in fact he still looked more like a gangster to her than a police officer.

She had to admit, though, that his car was not the type flaunted by the best gangsters, not Hollywood gangsters anyway. A mud-stained black sedan, it stood inconspicuously among its neighbors in the parking lot.

"Hope you don't mind sitting with the chauffeur," he said. He paid the attendant, held the front door for her with a ceremoniousness that was somehow distasteful, and said, "Allow me." But his foot was on the starter before she had time to settle back in her seat, and as the car merged with the thick traffic she hoped nervously that at least he was a good driver.

# 13

He was not, it developed, a driver who took his attention from the wheel to indulge in idle conversation. At first Addie was grateful for his dedication to the task in hand. It meant reprieve from the half-contemptuous, half-patronizing treatment to which she had been subject each time he opened his mouth. But very soon his silence became burdensome, coupled as it was with the car's slow progress behind trucks and taxis and busses and private vehicles. She regretted that she had not taken the subway and thought that the most crowded of trains would have been preferable to this snail's journey across town.

"Do we have far to go?" she said.

His grunt was unresponsive. He aimed it at a large and almost static truck directly ahead.

She repeated her question after the truck had picked up speed. This time he did not even grunt, and she assumed that her voice had been lost in the traffic noises.

She made no further effort until he turned the car into the East River Drive and headed uptown. Then she said, "Somehow I never thought of the Homicide Squad as being in this part of the city."

He did not answer, and she did not blame him. It had been an absurd remark considering the fact that she had never given the Homicide Squad any thought at all. "Is it far?" she asked for the third time.

"Don't be in such a hurry. You're not due for the red carpet when you get there."

The roughness of his tone startled her. She wondered if it could stem from what she had said in the office about finding someone with sense at headquarters. She set aside her jumbled anxieties to make amends.

"I'm sure you're doing your job the best you know how but——"

"You can say that again—without the 'but.'"

"Don't you like to drive?"

"Come again?"

"I said don't you like to drive?"

"What's the catch? Doesn't my driving suit you?"

"You do very well. It's just that you seem a little nervous. I know I'd be—with all that stopping and starting you had to do when we were crossing town. In Gresham I used to drive quite a bit, myself—and though the traffic there can't compare with——"

"You should have stood in Gresham."

She thought he had reason to be angry with her and so she forged ahead. "I'm afraid I lost my temper in that office. I'm sorry if I——"

"Relax—enjoy the scenery."

She sighed. She turned her head to gaze blindly at two companionable figures squatting on the deck of a garbage scow, at strong winged gulls swooping to penetrate with avid beaks the oily skin of the river. She thought her thoughts, weaving them into an opaque sheet that muffled sound and obliterated vision. She did not notice that the car was approaching the Queensboro Bridge. It was an alteration in the road's surface communicated by the car wheels that aroused her.

Her gesture of reaching for the door's handle was reflex. She had arrested it before he growled, "Sit still," making it sound more like a curse than a command.

She was not surprised. Neither was she frightened. It was as though the expected had come to pass. Nevertheless it had to be clarified. She straightened her back. She clasped her hands in her lap and said quietly, "But why are we on the bridge? I was told it connected with Long Island."

"You were told right." The peaceful nature of the question got home to him. His little spurt of violence petered out. He spoke with the air of a man who mops his brow after accomplishment. "Long Island's part of the metropolitan area—isn't it?"

Carefully she felt her way, willing serenity into her face and voice. "It's a shame police officers aren't exempt from parking charges. Does that come out of your own pocket?"

"Sure—sure. The police have a tough time." His oblique look seemed to be measuring her innocence. Apparently the result satisfied him. His smirk said that it was almost too good to be true. Clearly, since he had not counted on the bridge as being the least of his hurdles, he could afford to be magnanimous. "The police have branches all over the metropolitan area —Queens—Long Island—all over—but being such a well-informed lady I guess you were told that too."

She had been told something else, something much more important. But she had paid small heed to the inner voice that was her informant. This man had come to her armed with credentials, and she had been too uncertain of her own judgment to be governed by her distaste for him. Too uncertain or too stupid to read the signs that pointed to his spurious quality. But it was futile to think about that now. It did not matter how she had arrived at her present plight. It was what she could do about it that mattered.

The smirk clung to his thick lips. With relish he pursued the joke that he imagined to be unshared. "You wanted to talk to one of the higher-ups so I'm taking you to the Wheel himself."

His car was part of the long stream that flowed along the traffic lane. She was not really alone with him. She could attract attention easily if she so wished. Perhaps that accounted for the heavy calm she was able to invoke. Out of that calm her voice emerged, steady and smooth. "The Wheel? Do you mean the head of the Homicide Squad?"

"Who else?" He coughed to cover a laugh. "Happens he's visiting a Long Island precinct today—so there'd be no sense in letting you sit in his New York office until he got back. He wouldn't want that." Quite obviously he was experiencing a bully's pleasure in baiting someone half his size.

But I'll show him I'm not half his size, she thought. He's the stupid one. Not even a person as old and addled as he believes me to be would be taken in by that tale.

"Of course," he said, "the Wheel's apt to be burned you didn't bring the copy of Joe's letter."

"It's in a safe place." She marveled at her composure and prayed that it would not desert her. She had no doubt as to the identity of his Wheel, no doubt that he was taking her to Fix Watling. But the joke was on him because seeing Fix was exactly what she had set out to do. Only——?

They had left the bridge and were rolling along a wide street. He identified it for her in a mutter addressed to himself. "Once I get off Queens Boulevard I'll make headway."

She thought he had made enough headway, but she nodded submissively.

"Where did you put it?" he said.

"What?"

"The copy." For a moment he allowed his contempt to show, stripped clean of trimmings. "The c-o-p-y of Joe's letter."

"Not where anyone can get at it easily." She was heartened to see the downward drag of his hateful face. But she could not afford to indulge in minor satisfactions. She had a course to chart. Confronting Fix in a crowded office building was one thing. Being carried to him by force was another. In the office she could have controlled the situation with a threat or a scream. But what control could be exercised in the gangster's hideout that was surely her destination. She plucked that hide-out whole out of a film shown long ago in Gresham. It was a broken-down shack screened from civilization by rank foliage. It had two rooms, the larger an all-purpose affair containing a rusty oil stove, a shelf of canned goods, some rough-and-ready cooking utensils, and a wooden table around which mean-mouthed men sat playing cards. The inner room held the prisoner, bound and gagged, his eyes big with the effort to register terror. She thought inconsequentially that if she tried hard enough she would even remember the actor who had played hero-prisoner. James Cagney was it? Alan——? The sought-after face dissolved into the face of Lindsey. Her flesh prickled. Her own effort went into the concealment of terror. Not an actor but Lindsey. Not a film but reality. Reality in which she might never reach the place where her son was held, but be transformed en route into an unidentified body fished out of a bay on Long Island. Why did "bay" spring so readily to mind? She must have read it in the—— She begged herself to stop her nonsense; to keep her wits from wandering off in a maze of movies and newspapers. For if ever she needed a clear head she needed it now. Kate Barsony would have known what to do. Kate Barsony had the sense to go straight to the police when—— Jancsi! Was Jancsi a second prisoner, lying bound and gagged beside Lindsey in the hideout? Or had she been cast for the role of the beautiful sullen girl who swung her hips as she strolled on scene? Addie saw her leaning over the shoulder of a card player, wearing the look they all wore—all the movie sirens—nostrils distended—lips wet and greedy. But he pushed her away and rasped, "Not now, Baby. I'm busy," and it made her angry, and in the end—in the end—

What end? Addie looked out of the window. Not Queens Boulevard any more. Wan—Wanto—Wantagh? The street signs flashed by too quickly. But there were people and cars on Wan-something-or-other, and if she was going to scream or grab the wheel she had better do it before they turned into a deserted road. Yet Lindsey needed help and if only she could be sure that the hulk beside her did not intend to kill her along the way in order to spare Fix the nuisance of dealing with her, well then, she would take her chances. Where did the water begin on Long Island? On one of their trips to New York she and George had planned to visit a friend in a town called Southold. She remembered the name of the town but she could not remember why she and George had not gone. If they had, she would know when to expect the water—the drowning water that waited—— She wanted to lay her muddled head in her hands, but she sat sedate and still, evidencing nothing of conflict.

He was whistling. Would a man whistle whose mind was bent upon murder? Despairingly she recognized that thought to be as irrelevant as all the rest. He would whistle all right, or laugh or shout or dance a jig if the fancy took him. What was murder to him? He was the man who did the dirty work for Fix. He had beaten Joe Montheil to death, and had made her betray her son with her dreadful doubts and suspicions. He was—but wait—maybe he wasn't—maybe she was wrong. A man like Fix would have more than one henchman. This hulk could be just a scout whose duty it was to check for possible loose ends after the deed was done. Both his visit to the office, and to the apartment last night bore out that theory. Both came under the category of tidying up to make sure that nothing pointed to Fix. But suppose that last night she and Elaine had given him all the information they possessed? What then? She was back where she had started and he was the man who had killed Joe, and if necessary would have done away with her and Elaine. And he would do away with her now if it suited his purpose. Her hands gripped each other, kept each other from rising out of her lap in a pantomime of fear. Her hands were icy, gloved though they were, and the day so warm, and she in her winter coat. She must not show him that she was afraid. That would be the worst thing she could do. To avoid his sidelong glance she turned her head toward the window.

"It won't be long now," he said.

No matter what he meant by that it was too late to scream. Wantagh had joined Queens Boulevard in that limbo of past experience, never, for all she knew, to be relived. And this had happened while she sat in thought.

They were racing down a side road. It was not as deserted as it had looked in her imagination. Yet there was no one in sight who might serve as knight-errant. A young boy headed toward them on a bicycle. Watching his teetering progress she thought absurdly, I still think George and I were right not to let Lindsey have one when—— Oh Lord!

The car had missed the boy by the narrowest margin. She jerked around to see him sitting on the road's shoulder in a clump of marsh grass, the bicycle sprawled beside him. Forgetting everything else, she cried, "Wait—he might be hurt——!"

"Those little punks have nine lives—nine too many."

If she had needed further confirmation of his callousness, that was it. She hoped that the truck she had glimpsed in the distance would stop to see if the boy wanted help. She craned her neck, seeking for assurance in the rearview mirror. The boy and the bicycle were a far-off speck. The truck had dwindled to miniature size.

It was not the sharp pungent smell of clean salt air that braced her. It was conviction, sudden and strong, freeing her constricted heart, bidding it pump the blood back into her chilled extremities. He will not kill me—not until I've told him where I put Joe's letter. He will not feel safe until he knows where he can lay his hands on it—which means that I am safe. So long as I refuse to—what is the word they use—so long as I refuse to "sing" I am safe.

She saw the water then, a vast blue undulating body of it wearing ruffles of froth and spangled by the sun. And she could pay it the homage it deserved, knowing it was no enemy waiting to seize her.

The hulk was saying something. His false joviality came between her and the healing vista of beauty. "I guess you're thinking that just today the Wheel would have to pick an out-of-the-way precinct."

It seemed as propitious a time as any to end his nonsense. She said, "Don't be silly. What I'm thinking is when in the world we'll get to Fix Watling's hideout, Sergeant Leo—or is it just plain Leo?"

Fortunately he was a practiced driver. He kept control of the wheel, but he could not control his mouth. It gaped wide, as though she had hung a weight to his chin. She watched him struggle to close it.

"You old——!" Like a purist he searched for exactly the right epithet. "You old——"

"Not too old," she said, "to mistake you for an honest man."

His sense of humor rejected the joke that was on him. He shouted, "You had me pegged! You played along and all the time you had me pegged. You got any idea what could happen to you—you crazy old——" This time he did not search. The word came, bursting with its full measure of obscenity.

"That won't help," she murmured.

He glared into the rearview mirror. He pulled over to the side of the road. He braked with such force that she was thrown forward. His rough arm thrust her against the seat's back. "All right," he said. "Shake it out."

"I—I don't know what you mean."

"Don't give me that. You wouldn't be acting so cool unless you had something up your sleeve—something that makes you feel pretty safe."

She said simply, "I've got Joe's letter."

"You've got it—or you've taken it to the police? Which?"

She told a barefaced lie. "I've taken it to the police—and you'd better not try anything because they know just how the land lies."

"Did they tail you to the office? Are they——?" He bore down upon the handle of the door. He stepped out into the road and stared back at the empty stretch they had traveled together. Then he looked up at the sky, and then over at the water. When he re-entered the car he was eating his cuticle.

"They're not tailing you," she said, "so you don't have to be afraid of that."

He removed a finger from his mouth and gave brief inspection to its nail. His eyes shifted to the mirror again. He shrugged. He started the car.

She said, unable to leave well enough alone. "Just keep in mind they've other ways of catching up with you."

He said, "Oh sure. They're lousy with the latest equipment in spaceships and flying saucers—the invisible kind—and maybe the only way I can tell if I'm surrounded is to drop you into that puddle." He bobbed his head at the twinkling water.

"You'd better not." She tried to keep the words from quavering. "Fix wouldn't like it a little bit. If you know what's good for you you'll take me to him as fast as you can."

"If I know what's good for me," he said. "But all of a sudden I don't. All of a sudden I'm stumped." His voice lowered, becoming confidential. "Fix is a funny guy. Thing is he won't be expecting me to turn up with a package." He raised a hand from the wheel and loosened his collar. "Understand—I'm not asking for thanks—but I'm not asking for the treatment either—and with Fix you can't be sure—hell—I almost missed the turn." He gave the wheel a vicious twist. "Still and all," he said, straightening the car on yet another side road, "still and all—if I was to get rid of you without consulting him he'd flip too—so——?"

If he was worried, what chance had she? She said unwarily, "We don't have to go on. He wouldn't be able to do anything to us if we stopped and called the police and told them the whole story so that they could——" She bit her tongue. But in spite of the moisture that gathered in her eyes it was as though she had been gifted with X-ray vision. It was as though she could peer clear through the cloth of his coat to see his muscles relaxing. Hopelessly she told herself that she was gifted in no other way.

"Yeah," he said softly. "Yeah. And you had me believing the police *knew* the whole story. You really had me believing you'd gone to them—that it was only a matter of time."

"It is only a matter of time—and—and until that time comes I'll handle Fix."

"You'll handle——?" His face split to release a loud guffaw. "You'll handle Fix?" He choked on it. "This—this I've got to see. Grandma—you'll be the death of me yet."

With an intensity that lacerated her kind heart she hoped that his prediction would come to pass. Wearily she turned to the window again. Now there was no vista of beauty to alleviate her situation. There was only a straggle of frame buildings, the ugly tentacles of a town.

# 14

Town meant people, vehicles, another chance to do what she should have done at the outset of the journey. She wrestled with ways and means. Stealthily her hand crept to the device that controlled the window. It would be well to lower the window as much as possible in case——

He had stopped laughing. He was alert and very business-like. "Bend an ear, Grandma. You've kept on about wanting to see Fix—and you're such a card that I'm inclined to take your word for it—but if you should be thinking of changing your mind I got news for you. Budge from here on out—squawk one squawk—and it's going to be rough—not only on you but on any poor sucker who's close enough to listen. My gun's handy and I'll do what comes natural."

Her hand returned to her lap. The wordless answer satisfied him. He drove through the center of a town whose chief distinction was its lack of bustle. Most of the shopkeepers were taking the air in their doorways. Addie did not budge or squawk. It was no longer a matter of choice. She was irrevocably committed. A furious impatience seized her and she wanted to reach destination before the wavering ghost of her courage vanished forever. Each time the car stopped for a traffic light she had to clench her teeth to keep from crying, "Hurry—hurry!"

When the town ended, the car bumped up a long sloping dirt road. Here and there on either side of the slope she glimpsed an isolated roof top, and once a hound ran out of a thicket to bark at them. There was no other sign of life. Numbly she accepted the terrain as a fitting locale for a hideout. Therefore, the massive iron gate through which her gangster maneuvered the car seemed less real than any figment of Hollywood's imagination. So did the elm-lined driveway running between the soft green pile of wide lawns.

Her set lips parted. She said stupidly, "This? But this is somebody's private estate."

He muttered, "So we're living it up," and swallowed, and added sourly, "while we can." He did not look like a man who had ever burst into guffaws. He looked as though any expression of mirth was completely foreign to him.

The house was at least a quarter of a mile from the road. No one could have called it a shack. It was a two-storied structure, white with blue trim, and it rambled pleasantly over the landscaped grounds. There was neither man nor beast nor car in sight to show that it was occupied.

Evidently the hulk had been commanded to keep it that way. He made straight for the garage at the right of it, got out, and ordered Addie to stay put. He produced a key to the padlock, rolled the doors wide, and returned to the driver's seat. Not until the muddy sedan was placed beside a rakish sports convertible did he permit his passenger to leave it. Then he led her out into the air, holding fast to her arm while he secured the doors.

He marched her to the rear entrance of the house. That too had to be unlocked. It led on to an efficient kitchen, which in turn led on to a spacious hall centered by a modern staircase. Several doors broke the light pink walls of the hall, and through one of these issued a voice. Still holding fast to her arm, he pushed the door inward and took her with him over the threshold.

The room contained no oil stove or dour-faced men at cards. It resembled her preconception only in the close smoky quality of its atmosphere. Its main décor was books, shelves of them climbing to the ceiling. A thick gray rug covered the floor, and the rest of the furnishings consisted of a low desk with a large blank surface, a cabinet topped with glasses, bottles, and a siphon, a console radio-television combination, and a casual distribution of upholstered chairs and small tables.

Addie tried to gather reassurance from this unlikely setting and failed because of the figures standing near the console. There were three of them, two flat-bellied tight-belted men and Fix. They were listening to the radio. Its voice had covered the sound of the opening door.

She would have known Felix Watling anywhere. He was exactly as she remembered him, short and fleshy and highly glossed, in clothes designed to minimize his fat. There was only a minor alteration in his appearance. The last time she had seen him he had not been pressing a blood-flecked handkerchief to his cheek.

The men who flanked him wore good slacks and the type of shirts advertised as a gentleman's choice for country living. But somehow neither of them gave the impression that the country was their habitat. And this in spite of the fact that the first one to pivot toward the newcomers had the furtive look of an animal born to be hunted.

He nodded at the hulk. He blinked at Addie. His voice

came, filtered through his long sharp nose. "Hey—look—our Leo's here with his bride to be."

His partner had a pock-marked disillusioned face. It expressed nothing as he stared at Addie.

Fix turned off the radio. He said, "What's this?" He pointed at Addie but his frown was for her escort.

"Whistler's mother," the hulk said. Freeing Addie's arm he gestured at the ceiling.

It was enough for Addie. It was better than any scientist's dream of a youth serum. An agile white-haired sprite, she darted into the hall. She was halfway up the staircase when they caught her. "Lindsey—Lindsey!" she shouted. But it was a muted dream-like effort scarcely warranting the hand that was clamped over her mouth.

The sloughed years returned with interest as they prodded her back to the book-lined room. No sound came from the upper floor, nothing to indicate that Lindsey had heard or could have heard her scream. Dumped on a chair, she was glad enough for the respite of its arms. All hope and fear was suspended as she sat gasping for breath, trying to retrieve her sapped energies.

The focus of attention shifted to exclude her. Suddenly, Leo, the hulk, was picked out by a hard cold spotlight that seemed to have its source in Fix. The slacks-clad figures served as an audience. Implicit in their attitudes was the expectation that they would get their money's worth.

Leo plainly disliked the center of the stage. He did a little nervous footwork. He played to Fix. "Listen—there was nothing else to do. I could've fogged her but you said, 'Don't get fancy—do nothing without orders——' "

Fix had gone over to the desk. He covered a corner of it with his spreading rump. His polished shoes barely reached the rug. He said, "Did I give you orders to bring her here?"

"That's just it. But you didn't give me orders to fog her either—and the way it turned out it had to be one or the other. You sent me to check if she and the wife knew anything. So far so good. No stones unturned." He paused to oil his voice. "But even a man with your brains couldn't actually figure her to spell real danger—seeing there was nothing printed about Joe talking when she sat with him. Well—last night I'd have sworn she knew from nothing. Your name doesn't even come up though I dig my damnedest. But this morning was a different story. Between times she gets wind of the setup——"

"How did she get wind of the setup?" Fix dabbed at his cheek with the handkerchief. "Did you blow it at her—or is she on speaking terms with Joe's ghost?" The words dropped from his pursy mouth like pebbles.

"It wasn't me—and it wasn't his ghost. I had her eating out of my hand. Right up to the Queensboro Bridge I had her fooled——"

Fix said with devastating mimicry, "She was eating out of my hand—I had her fooled." He lowered the handkerchief and scrutinized it as though the blood smears were some indecipherable code. The wounds revealed were no more than a few scratches. "Why—if she accepted you as a detective—didn't you grab your diploma and bow out?"

The hulk switched from defensive to offensive. "It'll add if you let me tell it. This morning I go to the office like you said—to see is there any snooping around—and to pick up anything we could have left in our hurry. I find we didn't leave a thing that points our way—but that's later—after I take care of the painter——"

Fix swore.

"Well—what else can I do? He's on a ladder when I walk in—and he's started priming the walls for the next tenant. He looks good for the whole day. His back is to me and I got to do what I've come to do so I grab his legs and knock him out before he can see what hit him. Then I fine-comb everything. I'm ready to leave and get my lunch when I hear someone in the reception room and it's her. That's all I need—with the painter laying there and maybe waking up before it's convenient——"

Fix said, "Judging from past performance, I'll give you odds the painter will sleep forever."

"Huh? Now look—I told you a million times there was something phony about Joe pulling out when all I did was rough him up according to orders—so he'd think twice before he tried to step out of line again. As for that other job—you can't pin that on me——"

The sharp-nosed man in slacks had been grinning. He straightened his face. The moody expression of his companion deepened.

"Which reminds me," the hulk said. "If you're sore at me it's nothing to what you'll be at them when you see the papers. I got them in the car. I'll——"

"Stay here. I don't need the papers. I heard it on the radio——"

"Yeah but—say—I'm not criticizing—only is it such a hot idea to keep the cars under lock and key when we might have to make a quick getaway?"

Fix said quietly, "Have you cause to believe we might be compelled to make a quick getaway? Were you followed here by any chance? I hope you'll forgive me for asking."

"I don't know why you're leaning on me," the hulk said. "So help me I wasn't followed. I was thinking of the headless horseman——"

"How did this woman find her way to the office?"

"I'm leading up to it. I don't get excited when I see her. I'm still the detective and I worm her nice and easy. If I do say it I'm putting on an act that would——"

Fix seemed to puff out like a toad. The toad spoke in frightening accents. "You're asking for a pat on the back that you won't be around to remember. Are you going to fill me in?"

The slacks-clad figures were both grinning. Addie, who was breathing as normally as possible under the circumstances, heard the hulk's labored intake.

He took a running jump into his explanation. When the feat was accomplished, his little master made no comment. Without leaving the desk, he turned the hard cold spotlight upon Addie, wheeling toward her on his rump.

She said in a high voice, "How is your wife?"

"My——?"

"I'm not afraid of you, Mr. Felix Watling."

He studied her for a moment. Then his mouth smiled. "Of course not, Mrs. Prentice. I had forgotten that we'd met before. We're practically old friends."

"We're no such thing. You've got my son upstairs. I want to see my son."

"You've lived long enough to realize that few wishes are granted without giving something in exchange. And since you're here more or less at your own insistence you're undoubtedly prepared to strike a bargain. Where may we find this letter——?"

"I'll do no bargaining until I've seen my son."

The restless movements came from the other men in the room. Fix did not raise an eyebrow. "Has it occurred to you that your son might not want to see you—that your presence might embarrass him?"

"I'll take my chances on that. If you're hinting that you've got him to work for you I don't believe it. You ought to be ashamed—a man as educated as you trying to lead innocent youngsters astray with those ugly dirty books——"

"You *do* know a lot."

"I know enough to make me plain sick."

"I sympathize with you. You're going to need a great deal

of sympathy. In a few minutes Leo will be driving back to the city. We'll find the letter in your apartment, of course—but when Leo is searching for something in a hurry he's inclined to be careless—even a bit destructive——"

"I know how destructive he is," Addie said. "I saw what he did to the Montheils' apartment."

Fix said, "It's wrong to make accusations until you are certain of the facts." Then he said with an elaborate show of interest, "You're a widow, aren't you? There must be several reminders of your late husband that you'd hate to have destroyed. I suggest that you make it easier for everyone since the outcome will be the same in any case."

She had been prepared for maltreatment. The trivial nature of his threat surprised her and she was unable to prevent her mind from listing the few precious breakables that graced the top of her bureau. There was the bone-china pin tray that had belonged to her mother. There was the mirror that George had presented so charmingly, saying it would reflect the prettiest girl he knew. There was the pottery horse he had been so proud of because it was Lindsey's first try at sculpture. There was——

"Well?" Fix said.

She managed to look scornful. "Things—just things. Things don't matter." But unaware of what she did she stroked the watch upon her wrist because it had been a gift from George.

"Let me have that, Mrs. Prentice."

"Have what?"

"Your watch." He motioned to Leo, who took her arm and fumbled at the delicate catch.

"No—don't," she said. "It's nothing—it's like any other watch——"

An impatient tug severed the links, leaving jagged edges that cut her tender flesh. With the smugness of a reinstated favorite, Leo passed the watch to the little man. Addie tried not to look or listen as the pudgy fingers turned it over, and the unctuous voice read the inscription, "To my heart's queen, from George."

"An outstanding literary effort," Fix said. "I seem to recollect that when we met before you mentioned how much this tribute means to you." He dangled the watch by its broken band. "Perhaps you think I'm making a big to-do about nothing, my heart's queen—er—Mrs. Prentice." He did not look annoyed when the man with the pointed nose snickered. "In a way that's true since the letter written by the unfortunate Montheil is not important per se. The project to which it refers has been indefinitely postponed—so I have nothing to fear from the police on that score. You appear skeptical. Perhaps it would carry weight if I explained the reason for the postponement. There is a growing tendency toward censorship in this country which is nothing short of fascistic." His voice swelled emotionally. It ranged over her head, as though the books behind her were units in a listening crowd. "A Comic Magazine Association has just been formed to enforce what is termed a stiff code of ethics. The association has even elected a czar whose function will be to set the seal of approval on books *he* considers fit for consumption. Twenty-four publishers have been misguided enough to subscribe to this deplorable curtailment of the freedom of the press—not to mention five engravers—seven distributors, six printers—and a mat-making concern. Now—as you may have gathered—I am an individualist. I have never permitted myself to be regimented. Therefore, as matters stand, my field of operations is limited and I consider it the better part of valor to leave the youth of America to the milk and water diet from which I sought to rescue them until a more enlightened day when the red-blooded fare I prescribe is not looked upon as——"

"Garbage," Addie said dizzily. He had been swinging the watch—George's watch—like a pendulum. It was difficult not to follow its course to and fro, or to keep from being further hypnotized by the rabble-rousing voice he had employed; the sort of voice that could make even garbage sound important to a large and impressionable segment of the public.

Pointed-nose snickered again, nervously and out of turn. In the ensuing quiet he said, "You sound like a senator, Boss. But why waste it on her?"

Fix Watling did not reprove him. He wore the bemused look of a man who emerges from some sort of seizure. Then his eyes cleared. He dropped the watch to the rug and stood up to cover it with his polished shoe.

There was a small crunching sound that beat like a blast against Addie's ears.

"You may think it a waste," Fix said. "I merely wished to make my position plain in case our heart's queen believes she has some moral obligation to turn the letter over to the police. Not, of course, that she will be given the opportunity—but that she will be spared a great deal if she is co-operative. I am a gentleman and I prefer reasoning to violence—especially in dealing with delicate well-bred ladies who have attained to a ripe age without knowing what it is to endure cuffs and blows and nameless other insults at the hands of those whose only skill is violence." He stared meaningfully, first at Addie and then at the unprepossessing faces of the men. His stare bound them all together as participants in rites to which he would be but a detached observer.

Addie said on a thready note that miraculously held, "There had better not be any violence. You've been talking nothing but poppycock and I'm not interested in a bit of it. Joe's letter is important all right or you wouldn't be bothered to talk at all. And you won't get it—not if you break everything in my room—because it isn't there."

The odd thing was that, accomplished liars themselves, they did not suspect her of lying. She could read that in their eyes.

Their eyes did not credit her with any of the talents they esteemed and lived by.

Fix said sharply, "What have you done with it?"

"That's for me to know. I want to see my son."

"A monotonous tune. There are others who want to see your son—namely the police—and out of the kindness of my heart I've given him haven—even going so far as to extend my hospitality to his inamorata."

"His——?"

"Ah yes. She happens to be a widow like yourself—but not so faithful as to refuse consolation. Don't think too harshly of your son. Jancsi has a certain amount of appeal—and the pull of such affairs is too often stronger than a man's best instincts."

"It's not true. It's no truer than anything else you've said. He loves his wife. You're the one who's after Jancsi. I heard you—in the hall outside Joe's room—but she sent you packing——"

He said venomously, "Well—well—the ubiquitous Mrs. Prentice." Then, abruptly, he laughed.

She nodded. She was back in Joe's room. She was getting ready to leave and she was halted by that crude imitation of mirth; that lusty masculine laugh to compensate for the pasty flabby little creature he was. He could turn the laugh on and off at will whenever he found it necessary to save face.

He had turned it off. He presented his back to her as he went into a huddle with the men in slacks. Leo, the hulk, stood apart, looking uncomfortable, as though he feared the conversation might be about him.

Fix said, "Mrs. Prentice—my boys will take over now. I leave you with one ray of light. At least you're not being cut off in your prime—and at your age a few years more or less can't make much difference. Naturally, before you go, you'll answer the question dealing with the letter. To withhold that information would be spiteful and you won't want to depart with spite on your soul. You see—I have to know. Not—I repeat—because the letter is important per se—but because I cannot afford at this point to leave anything around that might bring me to the attention of the police. I won't bore you with the whys and wherefores. What it dwindles down to is the law of survival which unfortunately you neglected to invoke." He beckoned to the hulk. "Come along. They don't need you. You might grow too enthusiastic too soon."

Submissively, the hulk followed him from the room.

The slacks-clad pair waited for the door to close. Then the one who had been the silent partner muttered, "Windbag."

Pointed-nose said admiringly, "He sure don't run short of it."

"Could be we should start asking has he got anything else."

Addie's voice was a croak. "What do you think you're——?"

The two had advanced upon her. Pointed-nose said, "We're the quizzers—we ain't allowed to supply the answers—except by giving you a hint. Shed the shawl and bonnet. Make yourself at home." He tore off her hat and pulled the coat from her shrinking shoulders. "See what a swell valet I am. I'll hang them up real nice on the floor."

She struggled to rise and he laid his open hand against her chest. "You can't leave—you're the whole show."

Her lips moved soundlessly.

His companion said, "Take your hand away. Maybe she's ready."

"What's the matter—she remind you of your mother or something?"

"You creep! She's turned blue around the gills. Chill her before she gives and it will be a double funeral."

Pointed-nose removed his hand, but his presence was menace enough and Addie's eyelids fluttered down to shut him out.

She did not faint. She could hear her own heartbeat. She could feel her chest, tight and hot as though the heavy hand still pressed it. She could hear them conferring above her.

"You're as bad as Leo."

"I hardly touched her. She ain't seen nothing yet."

"I got no stomach for this."

"You're in a rut. Anything that don't call for a knife and you lose your nerve. Hey—Beautiful—wake up—let me put some roses in them cheeks."

The slaps stung, but indignity rather than pain forced her to open her eyes.

"You ready to talk?" He took the answer for granted. "That's the baby. Do my pal here a favor and spit it out before his ulcers pop."

She moistened her lips.

"You ain't saying nothing, Beautiful."

"You've scared her dumb is why. Being scared can clog the pipes."

"Jeez—I'm here to scare her ain't I?"

"Maybe a drink would——"

"And give her Dutch courage so's she can hold out some more?"

"Did I say it had to be whisky?" He went to the liquor cabinet, squirted some soda into a glass, came back and shoved it under her nose. "Try this on your pipes."

She drank too fast. The soda stung her nose and throat. She coughed convulsively.

Pointed-nose said, "If she can make that racket there's nothing wrong with her pipes."

Deliberately, she prolonged the paroxysm. She could speak all right, but why should she when her silence rendered them helpless? Only—the next time one of them touched her she would be unable to contain her voice. And if she cried out once they would realize that she had been shamming and there was no telling where it would end. I don't know how to be brave, she thought. I never had any reason to learn. And what does it matter? The letter is not important per se—what does per se mean? What does anything mean if I, Addie Prentice of Gresham, South Carolina, am really here at the mercy of these men——?

Overhead there was a series of crashes. Addie stopped punishing her scraped throat. The morose thug's head jerked back. He tried to stare through the ceiling. "What in hell——?"

Pointed-nose said indolently, "Pro'lly Leo digesting his lunch. To get back to business——" He leaned over Addie. "Now you got your throat clear maybe you'll cough up some sense."

She spoke. "Save yourselves."

"Will you get a load of that? Religion yet. Listen while you still got the machinery, Beautiful." His hand made a grab for her ear. "I'm going to——"

She crouched away from him. "You listen." She thought her voice was strong and confident. It was very little louder than a whisper. "It's not religion—it's the police. I didn't tell Fix but they know I'm here—and I'm giving you a chance to save yourselves by getting away before they——"

Pointed-nose laughed. "Why Grandma—what big lies you tell."

His companion muttered, "It wouldn't surprise me any."

Then both of them witnessed a change in her face that was almost transfiguration. They saw her rub her eyes, still blurred with the slapping and the coughing. They saw the eyes widen and drive through the space between them. Their bodies were rooted, but as the hunted will when frightened, they glanced over their shoulders.

The door had opened. Lindsey was in the room. His nose was bleeding. He had a bruise on his cheek. To Addie he was beautiful.

Her voice rang out as clear and strong as it had ever been. "Watch out, boy—they——" But the hands of her persecutors were arrested halfway to their pockets. They needed them to shield their faces from a blinding rain of uppercuts and undercuts and blows not included in the boxer's manual.

Behind Lindsey the dark detective stood, pointing his gun this way and that, unable in the confusion to aim. He shouted angrily, "I told you not to come in here alone, Prentice. I told you to wait for me, you outsized damn fool—they're knifers——"

Then he stopped pointing the gun. He said tolerantly, "Oh well——"

Addie was too busy to hear; too busy watching her hero in action, his face terrible and beautiful with honest rage as he wound up a truly inspired performance by knocking the villains' heads together. He had needed no gun. His strength was as the strength of ten because—— But what was she thinking of? "Lindsey—Lindsey—stop—that's enough now—that's enough."

And it was enough. The villains lay in a heap at his feet and he strode over them to come to his mother.

# 15

Lindsey's arms went round her and the gruff sounds he uttered were as tonic as band music. With her face against his shoulder she could not see the activities of the dark detective, who persuaded the country gentlemen to rise, and gun-pointed them from the room. When she drew away from Lindsey she was alone with him.

He stared in horror at the blood on her dress. "Mother——!"

"That's your blood, silly. Where's your handkerchief? Why Lindsey Prentice—that dirty thing—I've one in my bag but I don't know where—oh—I'm sitting on it—here."

With a hand that shook only a little she dabbed at his nose. "Is it still bleeding? A cold key——"

He grinned feebly. "You ought to see the other fellows. Are you sure you're not hurt?"

"Fit as a fiddle. I want to hear all about it—but you get on the phone first and call Elaine."

He no longer looked like an avenging angel. He looked like

a somewhat backward boy. "I don't know how to tell her——"

Addie, awash with questions, exercised restraint. "For a beginning I should think just the sound of your voice would be enough."

"Jancsi's using the phone."

"Oh?"

"At least she was. The minute we let her out she made a dash to call her mother."

"Wasn't she—wasn't she in the same room with you?"

"No—they'd locked her up on the other side of the house."

Addie said, "Oh," with a different intonation. She leaned forward and kissed his forehead.

He arose from his kneeling position beside her chair as the dark detective made a re-entrance.

"They're locked in the pantry," the detective said. "The baker and a local policeman are standing guard until the wagon comes." His tone was far from friendly.

Addie said timidly, "The baker?"

"I commandeered his truck just before the traffic thinned out. The squad car I started with wouldn't have tailed worth a nickel." He picked Addie's coat and hat off the floor and placed them on a chair.

Lindsey had not spent all of his aggression on the two gangsters. His hands were clenched. "You mean to say my mother led you here?"

"And lucky for you."

"You followed her in a truck. You could have stopped her from walking into this but you let her act as bait——"

"Your mother used herself as bait. I just took advantage of her foolishness." He stooped again to gather the fragments of the shattered watch. He eyed them grimly. "I wasn't the idiot who prompted her to——"

Addie held out her hand for the sad remains of the watch, doubly valuable because they created a diversion. "Please——"

"Huh? Well—careful—there are pieces of glass——"

She wrapped the fragments in the handkerchief that was stained with Lindsey's blood. She placed it in her bag. Out of the corner of her eye she saw both men watching her, saw Lindsey's fists unclench.

But something had happened to his deep voice. It squeaked. "Mother—I'll have it repaired. If not I'll—I'll buy you——"

She said tartly, "A house like this must have more than one phone. You call Elaine—hear? She's waiting on you." With relief she saw him quit the room before the moisture in his eyes spilled over. Then she tried to rise, but her legs were rubbery and she sank back as though she were merely resettling herself. It seemed important not to expose any further weakness of the Prentice clan to this cold young man.

She said, "I want to thank you—and I want you to know I wasn't quite as foolish as you thought. The man—Leo—posed as a detective—and for quite a while I believed he was one. Otherwise I wouldn't have got into the car. At least——"

"Maybe you would and maybe you wouldn't." He softened a little. "Your daughter-in-law skipped work this morning and came to Homicide instead—because thinking things over it occurred to her that he was a phony—and she worried he'd pay a return call and do you harm. That's why I was in the hotel when you left."

"Yes," she said, "I saw you——"

"I saw you too."

"You followed me? But I didn't—anyway not until hours later—and then only if you were in a truck I saw when I looked back."

"Could be. I almost lost you. A kid with a sprained ankle hopped into the middle of the road—and it was either stop or run him down. He was a smart kid with a beef and he'd memorized your license number. I loaded him and his bike on the truck and he directed me to the local precinct. The chief passed the license number along to some of the storekeepers so that they could keep their eyes peeled, and a gas-station attendant at the end of town phoned in to say what road you'd taken. The chief was also able to tell me that this place was the only one likely to house strangers. And what with a few more tags of information he provided it figured as your goal. I got here while you were in conference and planted the local cop outside the room while I cased the rest of the house. He had a job ducking a few unexpected exits and entrances but he made it. So you don't have to thank me. Even if you weren't in any real danger your nerves must have taken a beating."

She thought that something resembling apology lurked behind his ungraciousness. She said, "Well—I've got myself to blame. I should have consulted you in the Vauban lobby——"

"I should've too." He made another grudging apology. "But in my business a man gets pulled all ways for Sunday."

"You were in the office building when——?"

"Yes. I thought at first it was a waste of time—and except for your big boy friend it might have been. We'd cased the office the night before."

Complete deflation emphasized the lines of fatigue on her face. "I see."

He said awkwardly, "But you did put us on to this place quicker than we'd have——" He stopped. "What tipped you off?"

She told him about the hotel maid and the comic books and her discovery of Joe's letter to Fix.

He did not seem to regard it as the find of the century. He was at the desk, idly opening and shutting the empty drawers. He neither made comment nor launched more conversation.

She said uncertainly, "There's plenty I'd like to ask you—but I reckon we've caused you so much trouble you don't feel called upon to——"

"You've caused yourselves trouble. We might have had all this cleaned up yesterday if that hotheaded son of yours hadn't managed to crop off a first-class tail and disappear without a trace."

She said involuntarily, "I saw him yesterday."

"Not in the hotel you didn't—not since morning anyway—because we had Sandy there——"

She told him where she had seen Lindsey.

"Well I'll be——! And you couldn't bear to hurt his feelings by—never mind—skip it."

"You wouldn't feel called upon to tell me what Fix Watling was——?"

"Right now I feel called upon to see if there's anything besides rats in the pantry. There should be time to rustle up a lunch while we're waiting for the wagon. I haven't had a bite since breakfast." He added accusingly, "I'll bet that goes for you, too."

"Well—yes—but——" She glanced at her denuded wrist.

"It's about four-thirty," he said.

Jancsi ran into the room. Her violet eyes were as bright as they had been dull in the Ophelia phase. She was too excited to be surprised at seeing Addie. She addressed the detective in a husky compelling voice. "I tried the number you gave me but my mother wasn't there. She isn't at the hotel either. They haven't seen her since last night——"

The detective said, "Take it easy. She's safe." His eyes as he regarded her were less impersonal than his voice.

"Safe!" Slept-in clothes and tumbled hair did not detract from Jancsi's beauty. "Perhaps what you call safe. She left a note in case I got back before she did. I asked the clerk to read it to me. It said——"

"I know what it said. She told you she was going to the police—to confess to the murder of your husband."

Addie forgot her rubbery legs and they worked. She stood up. "Young man—if that's your idea of a joke——"

He said, "I hate to keep reminding you—but none of this is my idea."

She had turned to Jancsi before he finished speaking. "I saw your mother last night. She did say she was going to the police—to report that you were missing—not to——" Her voice faltered. She had put Kate's erratic behavior down to worry but——

Jancsi shook her head. "The note said what he said it said——"

"Nonsense." Addie's tone of reproof was for herself, Kate's friend, as well as for Kate's daughter. "The clerk made a mistake. Sometimes your mother's English is funn—is hard to follow. You mustn't believe——"

"I don't," Jancsi said passionately. "I don't believe anything—being kidnaped—or this house—or you—or him—or them—or—anything."

The detective looked at her. "Could you believe in a cup of coffee?"

"Coffee? Listen——" She planted herself before him, hands on hips, looking like a disreputable little gypsy. "I want to know why——?"

"I'm too hungry to hear a thing. Kidnaped or not you've been getting your three squares but——"

Jancsi said indignantly, "Three squares nothing. Fix tried to starve me into——" She flushed.

For a moment he was a study in controlled violence. Then he turned from her and offered his arm to Addie.

They met Lindsey in the pink hall. "I couldn't get Elaine," he said to Addie, "not at the hotel or where she works." Glumly he fell in with the procession.

A little while later they were seated at a table in a small cheerful dining room. The detective refused to answer questions. He keynoted the abstracted silence in which they ate bread and butter and drank coffee.

When at last he spoke it was with maddening inconsequence. "This isn't the best meal I've ever eaten—but it's the most bread."

"I hope it's restored your hearing," Jancsi said.

"Why—is there something on your mind?"

"No—not a thing—naturally not. I'm just wondering why we have to sit here waiting when there's perfectly good transportation in the garage."

"That perfectly good transportation might contain all kinds of evidence. We can't afford to disturb it."

"For heaven's sake—what more evidence do you need?"

"It's not what I need—it's the jury. But I guess that with kidnaping charges and confessions thrown in something ought to stick."

"My husband was murdered." Her face showed that even now she could not credit it. "And on that same day Fix forced his way into the apartment to make sure his orders had been carried out. So why should you have to throw in anything else?"

Addie, strengthened by hot coffee, joined forces with her. "It's true. I heard enough to convince me that the man they call Leo was responsible. He said he only meant to give Joe a beating—to teach him not to step out of line. You see—he'd knocked out the painter in the office and Fix seemed to think he'd killed him but he said he hadn't——"

"He was right," the detective said. "When I called headquarters I heard about the painter business. It was reported by the painter, himself."

"Well—that's how Leo happened to bring it up—about not meaning to kill Joe—but just the same——"

"Did he happen to bring anything else up?"

"I don't—yes—he seemed to think he was getting picked

on for nothing—so he mentioned another job and said they couldn't blame him for that. But Fix passed over it because he was in a hurry to know why I'd been brought there."

"What about the two men we found with you? Did they talk any?"

"They—they tried to make me say where I'd put the letter I told you about and—and one of them didn't like the way I looked—and his partner accused him of losing his nerve because he couldn't use his knife—something like that." She shivered, feeling the rude hand on her breast, the slaps.

Lindsey said protectively, "Mother—don't talk about it——"

"It doesn't hurt me to talk, Son."

The detective said, "It might even do you good. The more you talk the less you'll think later."

Jancsi raised her voice. "Psychology from cops yet." She sounded absurdly like her mother. "Painters—other jobs—knives! As if any of it adds or subtracts from the fact that Fix and his gang killed Joe."

The detective shook his head. "No jury will pin that murder on Fix. I doubt if it will even bring in a verdict of manslaughter because it can't be proved beyond reasonable doubt that the injuries inflicted by the beating caused your husband's death. If it came to a draw between Fix and your mother——"

Jancsi did not let him finish. She said incredulously, "It isn't possible that you're taking her confession seriously. I don't know what she could have had in mind. Maybe—maybe she thought I was involved or——" She searched each of their faces. Addie's seemed to provide her with inspiration. "Maybe even—well—Mother's taken a great liking to you, Mrs. Prentice. You remember how upset she was when I brought Lindsey into it. I know it sounds crazy but she's so terribly loyal that I wouldn't put it past her to confess just to divert suspicion from him."

Addie said a little coldly, "But he isn't under suspicion——"

"Hold it," the detective said. "You're all running away with yourselves. Mrs. Barsony didn't confess to save Prentice—even though he hasn't come out of this with flying colors. A fine deal for a grown man—let alone a schoolteacher to draw such——"

They all spoke at once, Addie in defense of her son, Jancsi in an attempt to clarify the matter of the confession, and Lindsey in desperation.

Lindsey, by virtue of being a baritone, got the floor. "The pictures I drew that night were as clean as the nudes exhibited in any public art gallery—not so good—but as clean. My host had started the ball rolling with an obscene and completely unskillful distortion of the human body—and because I was drunk enough to take my art seriously I had only one idea in my head—I wanted to set him straight about anatomy."

"Oh sure—and you were so afraid those nice clean pictures would be brought to the attention of the Board of Ed that you quit your job before you could get the heave ho."

The fight had gone out of Lindsey. His voice was only discouraged. "I quit because Montheil showed the pictures to friend Watling—and Watling thought they were real high-class stuff. In fact he was so impressed that he had them touched up to suit his needs—and then reproduced jumbo size—my signature and all—after which he held them over my head. Unless I was willing to talk business with him my teaching career was ended. Well—I wouldn't talk business so my career ended anyway—and who wins? I don't blame you for looking snowed. I felt the same way. Pornographic specialists are a dime a dozen—so why me?"

"Yes—why you?"

"I'll give you Watling's answer to the question. He said he had invested heavily in a comic-book outfit—and just as the books were ready to go to press the guy he'd picked to head the so-called art department walked out in a fit of temperament—

not only taking his staff with him but burning every scrap of the finished work. Watling said he hadn't time to hunt up another staff—but he assured me that he had no intention of losing his investment. Not when all I had to do to save it was gather a group of my best students together and step into the breach. He thought it would be a real break for the students. He'd pay them well and the money they earned would help with their future education. He's a great believer in education. He also takes the long view. He advised me not to choose students from one school only—but from each of the schools I supervise so that they could encourage distribution when the books came out. It was all very logical and he couldn't understand why I didn't go along with it."

The detective said, "What I can't understand is why you didn't go to the Board of Ed with it?"

"Even if I could have proved that I wasn't the perpetrator of the drawings in their present state of montage—do you think I'd be congratulated when I admitted not only to being drunk but to drinking with a companion like——" He glanced at Jancsi.

"Don't spare me," Jancsi said. "Just get everything out of your system so that we can return to the pitiful little unimportant question of who murdered my husband."

Lindsey had turned back to the detective. He said hurriedly, "In case you're too delicate to ask why I didn't take my story to the police I can give you several reasons. I didn't want to involve the innocent bystanders—and there was only my unsubstantiated word for the whole——"

The detective said, "Okay—I can see why you quit. But there are still things I can't see. For instance—how come we find you here?"

Lindsey said tiredly, "I'll be called upon for a full statement later, won't I?"

"In other words why should you waste time feeding my idle

curiosity—especially when you're so busy sitting here. I guess you wouldn't even care to explain why you broke into the Montheil apartment——"

"He never!" Addie said.

# 16

Lindsey awarded her with the ghost of a smile. "That's supposed to be a come-on, Mother. He knows I didn't break into the Montheil apartment. The idea is to make me piece together the rest of the sad story."

"Well—you aren't much of a hand at explanations but——"

"All right. I guess you rate one. Maybe I was too stupid to think of taking such direct action—though Montheil had told me he had custody of the drawings—originals and reproductions. But I thought Watling's boys had made off with them at the time of the beating. For a fact I didn't realize the apartment had been broken into until later—when Watling added it to the list of crimes that could be pinned on me."

"Where *did* you go that night when you got out of bed and——?"

"To visit Watling and try to make him surrender the drawings. Only I couldn't find him—and the next day in my lunch hour I went to the office he'd taken as a cover-up. You'd be surprised at how much can go on in a large office building——"

Addie was not surprised, but she did not tell him why. "Your lunch hour?"

"I'd got a temporary job with a construction gang—union card pending. I was doing fine—but what with the extended lunch hour——"

"Don't you worry. Your father always said you could turn your hand to anything. I'm proud of you—real proud. You'll have no trouble finding other work——"

They exchanged glances that shut the others out. Jancsi's voice intruded. "Maybe we could get back to the subject if I go on from where he left off. I was at the office, too."

"Why wouldn't you be there?" the detective said. "It was a rainy day and you had nothing else to do."

She turned a defiant face toward him. "I didn't think the police would ever get anywhere. I thought I could do better. At first I was sure Lindsey had given Joe the beating because—well—because there didn't seem any reason for Fix to be involved when he and Joe were so—so thick—and both of them working against Lindsey. But then—when the apartment was broken into—and left in such a state—pictures torn down—things smashed—it just wasn't what anybody related to Mrs. Prentice could do. So I decided it must be Fix after all. He'd given me the address of the office the day before in case I changed my mind and wanted to look him up. He said I'd got him wrong and he was a respectable publisher and could give me more than Joe could. So my idea was to pretend I—I had changed my mind. That way I could get him to tell the truth."

"Only you weren't very good at 'that way,'" the detective said, "or was it some other dame who scratched his face when he tried to cash in on the seduction act?"

Jancsi flung her arms at the ceiling. "I don't expect you to understand. No—I wasn't very good—but I had to try. A woman can't sit back and let her husband's murderer go scot free——"

"Okay—you tried. A trained squad armed with the best tools known to science was trying—but what did that amount to as stacked against your womanly wiles."

Lindsey said in disgust, "Stop needling her. If you're that desperate for entertainment I'll be glad to oblige. She barged into the office after I did—and she looked so cool I thought she was one of the gang——"

"Real farce material," the detective said. "Everybody mistaking everybody else for what they ain't."

"Do you want to hear it or don't you?"

"Proceed."

Lindsey proceeded. "Just before Jancsi appeared, Watling had informed me that the drawings weren't in the office. He said I was free to search if I didn't take his word for it—so I searched. Meanwhile he and his hoodlums stood around laughing. Naturally I turned up zero. Watling started to drip molasses. He said to run along and stop worrying because he'd decided to drop the comic-book deal. I didn't take his word for it. I had a notion to mop up the floor with him but the biggest of the hoodlums started playing with a gun—and Watling said did I want to make matters worse—and to prove his good faith he said to wait for him down in the street and he'd see what he could do about giving me back the drawings. So I went—only I didn't stop worrying——"

Addie, remembering his exit from the building, thought that he was understating.

"I guess," Lindsey said, "they took the easiest method of getting me out to the street under my own steam. They were pretty sure I'd wait for Watling—and I did—on the off-chance that he was leveling. And the next thing I knew the man with the gun coaxed me into a car and away we went."

Jancsi said, "Fix coaxed me without a gun. He played along

with my act and I thought we were going to some restaurant to get better acquainted."

"The abduction stunt seemed crazy," Lindsey said, "and still does. At first I made it that they couldn't afford to have us around loose—knowing what we knew about their racket. But the funny thing is I learned from what they let slip that they really have called a halt on the comic books."

"The rumor going the rounds," the detective said dryly, "is that you and Mata Hari had eloped—which stamps you as being in cahoots all the way—including Montheil's death."

Both Jancsi and Lindsey looked stunned. Addie said in what she hoped were airy accents, "Who cares about rumors?"

Lindsey recovered his voice. "But you said they didn't kill Montheil—so why should they have used us as cover?"

"Fix thought they killed him," Addie said.

The detective nodded. "Not that it bothered them. With you two runaway suspects to keep the police busy they were sure they could get away with it. And when the police had got tired of looking for you your lives wouldn't have been worth much either—unless you became members of their league. What did bother them was a recent development that could be laid to their door should the police hear your story and put two and two together."

Lindsey said slowly, "You've heard it. Can you put two and two together?"

"Like Einstein. You've been a help—all of you."

Jancsi became vocal again. "You're not a help. You're the most exasperating man——"

"Only when I'm working." For the first time he allowed himself to smile at her. "You should meet me socially some time."

"What about my mother—what about——?"

"Your mother and I would hit it off fine." He stopped smiling. "All right—I guess I've made my position clear on the subject of amateurs who risk life and limb when they pay a police force to do that very thing. For your information we were getting very close without assistance. We'd checked on Fix the minute he entered the picture and found him to be a bounced lawyer with a list of petty infringements against him —strictly small time as far as the record goes but—never mind —I meant what I said about you being a help. Still, if there's ever a next time leave it to us or your luck might not hold." He included Addie and Lindsey in the little lecture, but his eyes kept going to Jancsi's lovely stormy face. "Now that I've got that off my chest I'll give you a run down. The late Joe Montheil choked to death on his bridgework. Don't interrupt. It could have happened without the beating. So states his dentist who had warned him to take it out when he slept. It was a temporary job—an upper bicuspid where a gap would show if he grinned too wide. It was hitched by a piece of metal to the canine in front—but there was no molar behind to hitch it to because as a kid he'd been the victim of the pull-'em-out-when-they-ache school of dentistry——"

Jancsi cried, "Joe had a rotten life right from the start but he'd have hated this—this way of dying and having it talked about—worse than being murdered. He was so very vain—I remember when his own tooth broke off—at dinner—something hard he bit on—and he wanted it replaced in a hurry because it showed—and the dentist rigged that thing up and Joe was to go back and have a stationary bridge made—but it meant drilling away the back of a good front tooth so that it could be cemented on—or whatever they do—and he was afraid of the drill—he wouldn't——" She sobbed, "I couldn't get him to go——"

The detective inserted a finger between his neck and collar. He said, "Quit that—you wanted to know—didn't you? I thought you were a big girl and could take——"

"I can—but what's it to do with my mother or her confession—I——"

"I'm coming to it. Her confession doesn't amount to the meat in canned stew. She didn't like your husband—and I guess she got hysterical when you disappeared and felt it was some kind of retribution for what she felt about him. Happens in practically every murder case that people come forward with the damn—with stuff like that." He watched her as she tried to dry her tear-streaked face. Then he said casually, "Your ma will be here soon. Last I heard she'd dug the address out of the acting captain and was en route in a taxi. Why not beat it upstairs and treat yourself to a comb and a wash?"

Jancsi gave a little squeal and dashed out of the room.

He turned to Addie and said sheepishly, "I'm not used to dealing with such sensitive females. There was more to the confession than I let on but she just might not be able to forgive her mother if——"

"No," Addie said, "Kate didn't——"

"That's right—but when she entered the apartment and heard Montheil groan she went into his room. He was crouched over on the bed and she didn't stop to notice his lumps. She smelt the liquor and thought he was plain drunk and she was so disgusted she clunked him on the head with her pocketbook. For her own piece of mind we had her illustrate on the head of a convenient cop and the blow couldn't even have given a pigmy a bad headache. Besides—it wasn't a question of concussion. Montheil had been drinking when the thug got to work on him—and the thug doped the rest of the liquor in the bottle with chloral hydrate so that if he had an impulse to squeal when he got his voice back he'd sleep on it. Turned out the dose was too slight to take effect at once which is how come he could talk to you."

"Poor Kate," Addie said.

"She's recovered—but Homicide might not recover from

her. Anyway she's absolutely in the clear. Probably the thug broke the tooth the metal went round—only you can't fry a man for breaking a tooth."

Lindsey spoke. "What was the unexpected development that scared Watling?"

"Consult your newspaper." A frustrated sigh from Addie made him relent. "This artist who was supposed to have burned his work and walked out—well—he didn't walk out."

"Watling killed him?" Lindsey said.

"I shouldn't wonder. He was the owner of this house. The local police chief supplied me with that tidbit. Seems he'd made a commercial success—but his ex-wife is a spender and the courts were generous in awarding her alimony. No doubt Watling tempted him with a large offer and then reneged. At any rate a body was washed up early yesterday—not far from here——"

Addie said, "I—I read it—but it said—it said a decapitated——"

"Sorry, ma'am. Maybe you'd like to freshen up, too."

"No—please go on."

"It was decapitated all right—but it's been identified. It happened to be past alimony time for the ex-wife and when she couldn't locate her meal ticket she went to the authorities with a complaint. The description she gave led to the morgue where she was able to name the corpse even if he didn't have a head on him. He'd been operated on for a club foot—a thing that doesn't happen too often. He'd limped but he could get along without a special shoe—which is why Watling and Company didn't think to remove his limbs. Anyway—what with that and other familiar landmarks Mrs. Ex swears he was her wandering artist. Wouldn't you say it ties in? Now that we can get around to asking her the right questions I'll bet she even knows about the comic-book angle. She wouldn't care where his money came from so long as he handed it over."

"Headless horseman," Addie said, "something they mentioned about a headless horseman—like calling me Whistler's mother when they meant Lindsey's."

"Sure—every little bit helps," the detective said vaguely. "Weren't the chairs more comfortable in that other room? What say we wait there for the reserves?"

"I think I'd rather wait outside," Addie said. "I've been sitting too long and that room's so—so stuffy."

They were all standing on the front lawn when the taxi arrived. The retiring sun had left faint color forms in the sky. Addie watched their subtle alterations. In spite of the slight chill in the country air she felt warmer than she had felt in days.

Kate Barsony, stepping out of the taxi, was color too. She shouted, "Jancsi—my little bird," and Jancsi flew to her. They enfolded each other and drew apart and scolded and embraced again.

To give them privacy, Addie and Lindsey and the detective turned their backs and walked a few steps. They did not know that the taxi had held a second passenger until Elaine tapped Lindsey's shoulder.

"Mrs. B. and I teamed up," Elaine said, "when I went to Homicide to discuss last night's caller."

Lindsey had wheeled at her touch, but he seemed incapable of further action.

"Mother—are you—is everything all right?" Elaine said.

"Fine—just fine. And that—that thing we talked about—there was nothing to it—nothing."

"Well—he might at least tell me he's glad to see me," Elaine said.

Lindsey looked glad. Abruptly, he took her arm and led her to the rear of the house.

That left Addie alone, because several vehicles were rolling up the driveway and the detective was sprinting toward them.

But she did not feel shut out. Happily she visualized what was taking place between Lindsey and Elaine. He was a fine boy—and she was a fine girl—and they loved each other—and they'd make out. She'd help them. She had enough money left to tide them over until Lindsey got another job—and what else would she need it for with a strapping son like him who wouldn't let the grass grow under his feet—and when the baby came—then she would earn her salt all right. Elaine was probably telling him about the baby now—and he was receiving the news as George had received it—dark cheek pressed to fair—strong protecting arms tight clasped around her——

Kate Barsony joined her. Kate said reproachfully, "Addie—had you informed me you were coming to this place I do not permit you to come singlehanded. I also come. How long you have let me to idle my heels in that station house is not to contemplate. Do you think we will be lifted back to the city? If yes I will dismiss the taxi—for though your daughter-in-the-law shares—the price is to prevent cakes and coffee for weeks to come——"

Around them there was motion but little sound. Quite silently the prisoners were being escorted to the waiting cars. Kate sent a fierce glance at the pallid Fix, raised her handbag, and then lowered it. "Never mind," she said. "It is all over now. So we forgive and forget. Where is my Jancsi? Ah—she talks with that detector. It is a good sign. When the funeral is behind I invite him——"

Lindsey and Elaine were approaching. Addie saw that Lindsey wore almost as much lipstick as Elaine. She smiled at them, and it seemed to her that their answering smiles contained a lavish promise of the future.

Kate Barsony threw back her head and sniffed. "Spring must be on the next corner for already I smell it. Addie—if the weather keeps like today we will enjoy our sittings in Central Park—no?"